Greater Treasures

A DragonEye, PI Novella

I0540178

Karina Fabian

LASER COW
PRESS

Laser Cow Press

MERRITT ISLAND, FL

Laser Cow Press
Merritt Island, FL
https://fabianspace.com

Publisher's Note: This is a work of fiction. Names, characters, places, and incidents are a product of the author's imagination. Locales and public names are sometimes used for atmospheric purposes. Any resemblance to actual people, living or dead, or to businesses, companies, events, institutions, or locales is completely coincidental.

Cover art by Karina Fabian
DragonEye Logo by Len Fabian

Book Layout © 2017 BookDesignTemplates.com

Greater Treasures/Karina Fabian – 2nd ed.
Print ISBN 978-1-956489-09-5

Dedication

To Rob
My greatest Treasure.

*The greatest measure of friendship is not
what your friend would give up for you, but
what they would give you up for.*

Contents

Chapter One:
The Tail that Wasn't Mine

Imagine a world where technology and magic coexist, and humans rub shoulders with mystical creatures on a daily basis. Sound ideal? Forget it. The Interdimensional Gap opened between the Mundane and Faerie several years ago, and a lot of us Magicals followed the lure of a brave new world to settle here in Los Lagos—but just because we're bumping shoulders with you Mundanes doesn't mean all's well in paradise. More often than not, reality is as far away from ideal as your Hollywood versions of fairy tales are from Brothers Grimm.

"Coexist" makes a great bumper sticker, but it's not so easy when your kind are trying to kill me and mine—and now they have the access to weapons from two worlds to do it.

It was a lazy afternoon in early September. Lazy not by choice. Sister Grace and I hadn't had a case in over a week. I suppose I should have been grateful that no one was making trouble of a magical or demonic nature on our side of the Gap, but the electric and gas bills were coming due, and the only "job" we had was babysitting a couple of dogs while their owners were away.

We weren't even getting paid for that. The owner was a friend from church who promised to pray for us while on their pilgrimage. When I'd grumbled, Grace replied that I needed all the prayers I could get. Unfortunately, I could hardly argue with that logic. But I did remind her that as the apex predator in two universes, I had no problem eating them if I got too hungry or they got too annoying.

So the dogs were in the fenced run outside, and Grace and I were finishing lunch while watching the local talk show on the laptop. Los Lagos' own Geraldo-wannabe had invited a couple of Mundane Neo-Nazis and some Faerie toughs to discuss their differences. I wanted to be sure they hadn't included any of Los Despredatores, the neighborhood gang I've developed a kind of relationship with.

One skinhead had just finished announcing that once they had eradicated the "fairy contagion," they'd resume their crusade to purify the "proper" human race. I'd been betting the audience would storm the stage, when we heard the dogs barking outside.

I lifted my head to listen. "Customer."

"Just as well," Grace sighed with relief as she turned off the screen.

I pouted. "We didn't get to see the ruckus." As a dragon, I liked ruckus, especially among lesser mortals—and trust me, these guys were lesser. I felt my IQ dropping just watching them, and as large as my IQ was, it'd take quite a drop for me to notice.

Grace gave me a pained smile. She'd had enough anti-Faerie ruckus to last her a lifetime. The opening of the Gap had been a blessing/curse for her, too. Mundane psychiatry had been able to help her deal with the trauma of having been tortured by Satan's forces in our Great War. She'd spent five years in the D.C. area, far away from magic, while she was treated for PTSD. She might have even stayed there, never having anything to do with magic again, if it weren't for the fact that her part-siren heritage meant she needed access to a steady flow of magical energy just to survive. A little over a year ago, she'd returned to Los Lagos, working as a teaching assistant.

That was when her troubles began. She inadvertently used her magical gifts to compel a child to stop singing a particular song that (as it turned out) was a summoning spell for a Faerie demon. No one realized it at the time, however, and Addison Lukas, a complete drama queen (literally—she's a child star now) convinced the entire city and a good part of the Mundane populace at large that the mean Faerie had cursed her from singing at all.

Never mind that Sister Grace was a nun and a decorated veteran of our most horrifying war against bona fide, in-your-face evil. Never mind that Addison was a spoiled second grader seeking attention. Her lies made the news. Now Addison has her own sitcom while Los Lagos is still recovering from the riots and bad blood.

On the bright side, Grace got fired from teaching and joined my detective agency. She's much better suited to using her magic to fight evil, and she's the best partner and best friend I have ever had. I'd like to think I've been good for her, too, and she has pared down significantly on her medications, plus embraced her ability to use magic. We've saved the town multiple times—including from the demon that was summoned by that stupid song, anyway. People here had come to trust Sister Grace.

The change in housing plans for Territory hadn't helped things either. I couldn't believe how furious some people were getting over losing their new mall and hotel conference center. Apparently, FlintCorp's decision to change its development plans to create low-income housing for the community was "a slap in the face to the Los Lagos business community." The fact that an enchanted theater had inspired him to change his mind only added to the anti-Faerie sentiment. He'd had to double security around the first building site.

Fortunately for my people, that had only made Flint mad—and a mad Flint was a determined Flint. He pushed the rezoning and permits through in record time and was already breaking ground on the first site. And guess what? Grace had been instrumental in that happy occurrence, too.

Even so, she felt guilty, like her actions had single-handedly caused the anti-Faerie sentiment. In addition to watching out for my favorite gang members, I had wanted to watch this show to prove to her that the hate was already there before she showed up and would continue long after she was gone. Mundanes, like most mortals, had this annoying need to identify themselves as standing against another group. The Faerie were just the latest "them" in the "us vs. them" mindset.

Addison had simply been a convenient rallying point, and her repenting could not stop the wave of animosity. It flowed as inexorable as magic, seeking its next leader.

Our job, then, was to be sure that the next leader didn't have a chance to rise. That was the third reason to watch, but no—no one on *Benson Today* had the leadership skills or charisma to lead more than a handful of idiots wielding chairs.

"I think we've seen enough," Grace told me. She went to the window and peered out the miniblinds. "She's good with the dogs—friendly, but not gushing over them. Nice outfit—business, but not too out of place. Sensible shoes. Her hair's redder than mine."

The window was partly open, so I used my sniffer. "Out of a bottle. She's got money, too. More than you should carry around in this part of town. Good thing, too. Bills are due."

"I need some supplies for the workshop, too, and the arcane market isn't interested in any more of your scales or urine."

Every part of a dragon—from fangs to fewmets—has some kind of magical value and is highly prized by mages in Faerie. St. George had taken most of my grandeur and magical capabilities from me with his spell, but there was one thing he couldn't mess with, and that was a natural reaction of dragon digestion. I didn't mind filling a few bottles to sell, but of late, we'd flooded the market, so to speak.

Last year, we'd solved the case of the haunted theater and she'd been about to pull the magic she needed from the Gap directly to our lair and her workshop to feed her spells. Now, she was working on creating charms that would protect us and others—charms for stealth, for healing, for protection. Unfortunately, it seemed that we used her supply as quickly as she could create them. Right now, the limiting factor was supplies, which required money.

In the meantime, she'd devised a spell so that if the flow of magic was diverted, she'd get an alert and we could investigate. Just another way she's made everyone's lives safer by embracing the magical talents she'd shunned after the war. I was coming to depend on her abilities as much as on her companionship.

Which meant I had a vested interest in her well-being. I'd already chased off the demon that had been snooping around when we first met, hoping to bring her ruin. Ironic how that had been easier than dealing with the creeping poverty that was the mainstay of our current existence. Never mind magical items—we needed a job, or she was going to have to go to the food bank while I wandered around the neighborhoods, snacking on rats.

"Here she comes," Grace said and took her place at her desk. She used a cantrip to open the door just before our stranger touched the doorknob. I avoided smirking. I didn't know if it was our potential client's red hair or Benson Today that had my nun's ire up, but regardless, I always enjoyed it when she showed off a little.

"Welcome to Dragon Eye Private Investigation Agency," I said as our guest stood at the threshold, her mouth open in a dainty "oh!" of surprise. "I'm Vern and this is Sister Grace. What problem can we solve for you?"

Grace indicated a chair, and she sat hastily, perching on the edge. Her hair was a golden red; someone went to a lot of trouble to get rid of all those dark roots. Brown contacts hid her blue eyes and made them look mysterious and innocent. She had one of those figures that was popular with Mundanes today—curvy without being hour-glass—her legs half-hidden under a tight skirt she seemed accustomed to without actually liking. She clutched a carefully-not-too-expensive pock-etbook in front of her. Her nails were short, pink, and fake. She was trying to look scared and un-sure, and doing a fair job of it, but you can't fool the nose of a predator.

"My name is Eva, Eva Heidler, and I need help. It's my brother, Weylin. He's gone and joined some cult. I think it's called the Brotherhood of Baal?"

Grace and I exchanged longsuffering glances. "Baal?" I sighed. "You know, I realize there's a lot they don't teach in Mundane schools, but you have science fiction shows. A couple of episodes of *Stargate*, and anyone'd know he's bad news. They got that much right."

It never ceased to irritate me how Mundanes refused to understand Magicals. It's been nearly a decade since the Gap opened between this world and mine, and people still think catching a leprechaun will get them gold and not a debilitating curse. Many of our worst cases started out with some idiot thinking the supernatural realm held the answers to all their problems. Looks like we'd just gotten another one.

Grace set a hand on my flank, both to show her sympathy and to prevent me from a rant. Alienating a client would lose us a case, and we needed the money.

She said, "I'm sorry to hear that, Miss Heidler. How can we help?"

"I've been trying to get to him, but he's in some kind of isolation, probably because of me. I found a man who said he can arrange a meeting, but only if I... He wants me to..." She reddened and didn't finish her sentence. "I thought, maybe, if you'd take the case, I could meet him, put him off one more day, then you could follow him, and he'd lead you to my brother?"

"Why not hire a Mundane for that?" I asked. Usually people only came to us for problems that required our unique skills.

She bit her lip. "Well, I think he's part of the Brotherhood, and given how he was acting... And things Weylin said. Could it be the actual Baal?"

"How much do you know about this cult?" Grace asked.

"I don't. I just know a couple of weeks ago, he'd made some new friends, and they kept talking on and on about Baal. How he was going to solve all our problems. Last week, he came home with a tattoo. 'Brotherhood of Baal.' Two nights ago, he was gone. Our parents died a couple of years ago, and I've been trying to do the best I can, but... Please, find him for me, and I'll get him all the help he needs."

Her eyes filled with tears then. Nice touch.

"When are you supposed to meet this man?" Grace asked sympathetically, though I don't think she bought the story much more than I did.

Eva gave us the address of the hotel and the time she'd be in the lobby, then pulled out a roll of bills from her purse. Tremblingly, she laid them out, a combination of Faerie and Mundane, watching for some signal that it was enough. I let her lay out the price of a couple of her expensive perms and manicures before I leaned forward and pulled them toward me.

I said, "Don't take any notice of us tonight. We'll contact you when we have something."

⚖

Rather than promoting greater understanding between the Faerie and Mundane "races," Benson Today's little stunt only aroused the ire of the locals. Faerie, especially Magicals who didn't look human at a glance, were cautioned to stay off the streets. My contacts weren't the kind to be seen hanging around when the police were on alert, so Grace and I did internet research into the Brotherhood of Baal but didn't find anything useful.

Unfortunately, that only helped Eva's story. If Baal, the actual Faerie empyrum, was loose in the

Mundane and starting his own cult, it would probably not be widely advertised until he felt comfortable in his power. He'd already taken on the Christian forces in the Great War, and for once, the fertility god's efforts had not been fruitful at all.

That evening, Grace came down from her room looking far less comfortable in her thrift-store slacks than Eva had in her expensive skirt. She wore a light jacket over her sweater and under it, her guardian angel medallion. She'd replaced her wimple with a brown wig.

"Well?" she asked, doing an awkward spin in her sneakers.

"Very Mundane. But I still think I should go alone."

She didn't protest the logic of a 12-foot quarter-ton scarlet-and-black North African Faerie Wyvern trying to discreetly tail anyone in the streets of Los Lagos. I'd been at this job for years before she joined my detective agency. I'd done everything from finding lost cats to solving murders—and tailing suspects. As a predator, I could be very stealthy. I could hear and identify a person's footsteps from two blocks away, and my eyesight was magically enhanced. Plus, I can fly. Very few Mundanes look up when they suspect someone is following them.

Even so, Grace was my partner now, and it was true that she could move in areas I could not, like the bar where Eva was supposed to meet her contact.

Still, I didn't like it.

She picked up my thoughts. "Do ye still have a bad feeling about this?"

"She's unicorn bait."

"Aye, I think so, too." She sighed. "But if there's a cult of Baal brewing, the Church needs to know. Especially now, with tensions between the Faerie and Mundanes so high, which is another reason why I have to go, too."

"Just... Be careful. Follow him, don't get seen, and call me once you find his hideout. I wish you'd had time to finish your stealth charm." We only had one left, and it was attuned to me.

"Vurnerrah," she said my given name in as close to perfect pronunciation as any non-dragon could. "This isn't the first time I've skulked about in the shadows. I was actually rather good at it once upon a time. In the Great War, I worked behind enemy lines a time or three. I think I can handle a simple tail job."

"A time or three?" I asked skeptically.

She paused to think. "Three times. I was captured on the fourth. I suppose I got overconfident."

"Well, don't get overconfident this time," I warned.

"I promise. I learned my lesson," she told me.

It was the last thing she'd say to me for a long time.

Chapter Two:
A Shot in the Dark

One thing I have come to appreciate in the Mundane is your communications technology. True, it makes it easier to spread lies, as it had when Addison accused Grace of cursing her, but it also meant that I could keep in touch with Grace during the mission.

I was hanging out on the roof of a building about a block from Eva's hotel, the closest building that both gave me a view of the hotel while affording me a place to hide. I had half an eye on the doors and the other on my phone as Grace and I texted.

My perch had a great view—"great," in that I could see the hotel and as far as Territory. What I saw, however, was far from inspiring.

The roof behind the hotel hosted a billboard for Addison's new sitcom, treating me to a six-foot picture of her face. Same bratty expression, more makeup. Someone has graffitied it with "Don't Forget" and the symbol for the anti-Faerie movement: a blunt F with a triangle growing out its back to make the A. Beside it, there was a stylized swastika. Don't forget. How much had the vandal forgotten to be able to inscribe all that without irony?

The protest at the TV station in front of the City Center was finally breaking up. Most likely, the news crew had finished filming and the more genteel of the crowd had decided it was time to get a late dinner or a latte at one of the nearby restaurants. I noticed the neighboring stores were open. Did protestors go shopping after?

I wondered if Owen had changed the display at his comics shop again. When all this started, he'd ordered extra copies of every issue that dealt with mutant racism and set them on sale in racks at the front. He'd gotten his window smashed once, but since they'd stolen some of the comics, he'd said he was going to hope they were read and count it as a win.

I texted my report to Grace, along with the comment about Owen. A moment later, I got a reply.

Owen is a good man. I hope someone just buys comics this time.

Looks like some of them are taking their march to Territory.

Do you want to go?

I thought about it. Those were my people. I'd scratched my mark on their walls and vowed to protect them if I could. Still...

There are some uniforms following them. Maybe they'll stick to motivational speeches.

You sure?

Santry would probably arrest me for breaking curfew, anyway. I'll keep an ear out. How's our mark?

He and Eva are just talking. She tried to give him money. He made a pass at her instead. At this rate, I may have to order some food to go with my wine.

Did you check the wine?

Yes, Vern. This nail polish is an amazing find. I was thinking I might be able to alter it to detect magic potions, too. Wouldn't that be handy?

A tracking charm would be handier.

It's on my list. Anything on the photo I sent?

Nope. This guy operates off the grid or has changed his appearance somehow.

Well, if nothing comes from tailing him tonight, maybe we can ask Michael.

Maybe *you* can. Captain Santy isn't doing me any favors. He has a thing against me. I'd swear he was a knight in another life if I believed in that sort of thing.

☺ Maybe if ye didn't act so superior.

I am superior!
You're teasing me now, aren't you?

Hang on. He's handing her
some paper. Get ready in
case this is when he leaves.

I was smirking, imagining how she would reply, then a rumble shook the air, followed by distant screams.

Was that thunder?

No. Explosion. From Territory.

Go!

Vern, go! I've got this. I'll be fine.

Now I could smell smoke. An apartment building—one with a mix of Faerie and human tenants—was on fire.

Tell me you're on the way.

I'm going! Be back as soon as I can.
BE CAREFUL.

You too. 🙏

I launched myself into the air, cursing the timing and saying my own prayers for anyone in the building and for my partner. I passed the fire station on my way. They were just pulling out. By air, I'd get there before them.

I arrived to find the locals already in action—or at least the Faerie-born locals and those Mundanes who could be shamed into helping. The rest stood well away, watching fearfully or recording the incident on their phones. Meanwhile, those that had the backbone to match their hearts were attacking the flames with hoses. It was a hopeless battle. This was one of the oldest buildings, so out of code, it had been condemned, which only meant that it'd been taken up by squatters and hoarders who had refused to leave and a couple of families who were going to stay as long as the vagrants did. The fire had plenty to feed on and was growing fast.

There were still some people racing from the building. Some even jumped from the higher stories; I saw a centaur on the ground, his arms wide, trying to convince a frightened woman that he'd catch her. She stood on the ledge but could not make herself jump.

I swooped down, nabbed her in my claws, and dumped her in a yard across the street. Without waiting for thanks or curses, I went back for the next trapped person. I heard a child's screams on the third floor. I lowered my head and rammed the closed window with my horns.

I found them in the second room. The mother had passed out trying to grab the baby. She slumped over the crib while her toddler son shrieked, and the older boy pulled at her skirt and begged her to wake up. Neither had noticed the flames crawling up the wall.

"Kid!" I yelled. "I'm getting you out of here. Climb in the crib."

He stared at me.

I growled. I expected too much. I scooped him up and plopped him next to his baby sister.

The bottom of the crib dropped out. Fewmets.

Fine. I wrapped my tail around the toddler and scooped the unconscious baby in my mouth. Then I rose, grabbing the boy in my back claws and his mother with my front. My wings strained against the awkward load in such close quarters, but all I had to do was soar down gracefully enough to not hurt anyone.

The window was too small.

The flames had followed me to the room, fed by the air coming from the window. I didn't have time for two trips. I set everyone down and smashed out the rest of the glass and the frame of the window. The boy scooped his sister and little brother in his arms and watched fearfully. I flared a wing over them to protect them from the heat.

"It'll be okay," I told him. "We're getting out of here right now, but you need to be brave. You get to ride the dragon. How cool is that? But you have to hang on tight, okay?"

I settled down low and told him to climb onto my back. His brother tried to climb on, too, and screamed when I snatched him with my tail. "Sorry kid. This is safer."

Again I took baby sister in my mouth. With all four limbs to hold mom flat against me, we could just fit—if I held my wings in tight and jumped.

"Lean in. Hug me hard!" I told the kid. I folded my wings over him for protection. Then, I applied a little magic, levitated, and propelled myself forward.

Mom's dress snagged on a jagged piece of the window frame, throwing off my balance. My wings scraped the broken glass on the top of the window, and I tumbled forward. I fought not to clench my teeth against the pain.

I did not have time to open my wings for a soft landing.

I ended up crashing to the ground on my side, trenching someone's grass and taking out their lilac bush. As leaves fluttered around us, I spat out the baby and gingerly opened my wings. The boy tumbled out, crying and grabbing his elbow, but immediately ran to his mother and started to shake her. I settled baby brother, who has passed out from smoke or fright, beside them.

The fire department had finally arrived.

"Hey!" I called out. "We have injured here!"

An EMT ran up to us. She looked them over, but when she came to the now-screaming baby, she made a face. "Did you have her in your mouth?"

"My hands were full," I snapped. "She needs a diaper change, by the way."

I shook myself. I was scraped but otherwise fine. I took off to find my next rescue.

Twenty minutes later, the building was empty, the fire almost out, and the injured seen to. I landed in a yard across the street panting. My claws ached from grabbing people. My wings hurt from the cut glass. The worst of it, though was the soot. It had gotten oily and – weird, somehow – and now it was under my scales. I needed a bath, bad. I rolled in the grass, trying to wipe the worst of it off. The dwarf that owned the house saw me, hollered for me to stop ruining his lawn, then sprayed me down with his garden hose.

I'd just shook myself and thanked him when the EMT found me. She had a bag of medical supplies in her hand.

"A lot of people are going to be okay, thanks to you," she said, setting the bag down beside me, "including that family. Now, let me see your wing."

I unfolded it, wincing. "Be quick. There's someplace I need to be."

Just then, my phone rang.

"Vern, it's Kel—Officer Killian. We found Sister Grace in an alley."

"Is she alright?" Of course, she wasn't. The police would not be calling me if she was okay, but the words came out of my mouth like a bad script. Kel's answer was worse than I expected.

I launched myself into the air so fast, I knocked over the EMT.

Ten minutes later, I was standing at Grace's bedside at Los Lagos General, trying very hard to keep from bumping the various tubes and machines they'd attached to her to keep her alive. Kel Killian was with me; there'd been a uniform outside I didn't know but who looked mighty suspicious about a dragon entering his good Mundane hospital. Bet he was one of Santry's favorites. He'd followed me in and was eyeballing me warily from the door. The doc was giving me the evil eye, too.

I dunno. Maybe it was because I was bedraggled, still kind of sooty, and smelled, if not of brimstone, then an equally nasty combination of burning trash and building materials. Not the most sanitary look for a hospital visit. That's what Grace probably would have said. If she could say anything.

Still, everything felt wrong, even given the situation.

I turned my attention off myself and my ire and to what Kel was saying.

"It was sheer luck we found her. There are always screams in that neighborhood, usually domestic disputes, and most of us were busy with the protests and the fire. We might have ignored it, but this lady kept calling insisting it was different. Then Sadie—Officer Velasquez, one of our rookies—passed by the area without noticing anything but came back because she said she had a funny feeling like someone was leading her."

I pulled down the collar of Grace's gown with one claw. Out of the corner of my eye, I saw Uniform's hand reach for his sidearm—like I was the threat to my own partner. "Not luck. Where's her pendant?"

"Her what?"

"Guardian angel pendant. It probably saved her life." I was about to chew the lot out for divesting a mage of her protections when Kel smacked his forehead, muttered, "Oh, right," and dug through the closet.

Father Rich snuck in just as he found it, squeezing past the uniform and giving him a chiding look. Uniform's hand dropped from his sidearm to his side.

"I came as soon as I heard the news," Father said before crossing the air over Grace and murmuring a prayer. Kel handed him the medallion, and he held it out in his open palm toward me. I set my clawed hand over his.

Together, we murmured a prayer to reactivate the spell. I felt a slight tingle of magic, but it was weak. The magic faded even as I watched. The charm had been totally sapped. Nonetheless, I felt marginally better—or at least, not as wrong anymore. I still itched. I still worried.

Father Rich put the chain back on Grace's neck, careful of the ventilator.

"I doubt magic will help her," the doctor noted with professional pessimism. "She was shot with a dart gun full of poison, animal tranquilizers, and iron."

I jerked my attention from Grace's too-still features to look at Kel. He held up his hands to show me the size of the dart. Big enough to take down an elephant.

Or a dragon.

I answered Kel's questions: Yes, she was on a job; I texted him the photo of the perp she was trailing and told him when she'd left the hotel but didn't reveal our client's name. No, I didn't know who might have done it. There were plenty of folk, Mundane and Faerie, who didn't like me—seriously, take a number—but most were smart enough to tell a human from a dragon, and most knew an error like that would only make me angry, and they wouldn't like me when I'm angry.

Kel answered my questions: No, no eyewitnesses, just a lady who heard a scream. No sign of struggle. The needle on the dart was made of titanium, which would pierce through my scales nicely. Shot in the back from far enough range that it broke a rib and bruised the surrounding tissue but didn't damage any internal organs.

When the doctor was less than forthcoming about his patient's—my partner's—condition, Kel supplied those answers, too, while the doctor blustered about "patient confidentiality" and how there was no use telling an animal, anyway.

"We need to speak to her next of kin," he protested. "There are decisions that need to be made."

Decisions. What a careful euphemism for whether or not they should just stand back and let Grace die. It was a good thing Kel stood between us. I was ready to lose my temper and act like every bad stereotype Mundanes had about dragons—including making a meal out of the doctor. It seemed only fair considering how he was acting like every bad stereotype of an arrogant physician.

Father Rich set a hand on my flank and spoke calmly to the doctor about contacting her order in Faerie. "In the meantime, I think you'll find that Vern and I are listed as her emergency contacts."

He peered at me, doubting whether I could be considered a viable contact, but he seemed to decide that he was outnumbered. "There's some paperwork that needs filling out, including the contact information for whoever has decision authority on her behalf. I'll have a nurse bring it."

The room felt more peaceful when he left. Kel made his goodbyes at that time, too, promising to let me know if they found anything more.

Officer Uptight stayed, but his eyes were flickering between us and the television that was playing in the background. Why would anyone even have that on? Did they think Grace wanted to see the news?

Then again, the anchor was talking about the fire. Maybe the staff had it on to know what to expect?

"That you?" The officer jerked his head at the screen.

I looked in time to see a very nice shot of me carrying a guy off the roof. He was a tramp, sleeping up there to enjoy the cool air, he said. Considering he'd vomited on my foot, I suspected he'd been enjoying a bottle or two of cheap hooch.

"Must be," I said without any graciousness. "I am the only dragon around."

"Where were you when the fire started?"

Stupid me. I thought he had planned on commenting on my heroism. "Halfway across town, where I was supposed to be backing up my partner."

He made a noncommittal grunt.

"What does that mean?" I spun to face him directly, cheek crests flared, eyes flashing, claws digging against the floor.

"Vern," Father tried to soothe me, but I was not in the mood to be mollified by a priest. I wanted an apology or a fight.

Just then, the nurse stepped in. I recognized her from Little Flower Parish. She took one look at me and at the officer.

"This room is too crowded," she declared, then pointed to the policeman. "If you're here to guard Sister Grace, then I'll thank you to do it from the hall, please."

Like the doctor, he at least had the good sense to know he, too, was outnumbered. He gave the nurse a curt nod and left.

The nurse shut the door behind him, shut off the TV, which had returned to discussing the anti-Faerie violence in the area, then turned to us. "I'm so sorry about all this. We're going to do everything we can for Sister Grace. You know that, right?"

I wanted to believe her, but the doctor and the paperwork, asking about insurance we didn't have and responsibility for bills we couldn't pay, did not inspire confidence. I filled everything out, anyway. Then I stuck around long enough to pray the Sorrowful Mysteries with Father Rich before taking my own leave. I wasn't going to make Grace better by worrying, and there was only so much my prayers would do.

As I left, I took note that no police officer stood guard in the hallway.

Chapter Three:
Dead Ends and Half-Truths

It was just after four in the morning when I took off, with a cloudy moonless sky, but I wasn't taking any chances. I activated the stealth charm Grace had made for me after watching a documentary on the B-2 and headed to the scene. Around me, the light curved and diffused, so that I was at most a ripple in the night sky. Maybe on a bright, starry night, someone'd notice, but tonight, the baddies would have to be using enhanced sight and actively looking for me, and even then, the odds were in my favor.

I circled the neighborhood where they'd found Grace, my own superior senses straining to pick up anything unusual while the rest of my brain mulled over motives and suspects.

There were plenty of people (and I use that term loosely) who wanted to see me dead—and even more who knew I was an immortal creature, who wanted me out of commission for a long time. Since the Gap had opened up between the universes and I'd hung my shingle in this one, I've ended up saving both worlds many times, even before I'd teamed up with Grace. And after every Save The Universes Case, there seemed to be more beings who promised their revenge than who were grateful. To add insult to injury, those who were grateful seldom made an effort to show their gratitude tangibly. They say crime doesn't pay, but inadvertent heroism doesn't satisfy the electric company, either.

Or the hospital. How many of those "decisions" that Doctor Doomsayer wanted to make were financial in nature? I had a cave of treasure in Faerie. I was banned from using it for my own purposes, but surely Bishop Aiden would make an exception for Grace's life.

I shook myself and brought my attention to my senses. Nothing stood out to me on the way to the scene of the crime, nothing to indicate a hasty getaway or a planned ambush. I landed on the roof of the building over the alley where Grace had been found and turned my mind back to motive.

Most of the vengeance types weren't this sloppy. They would have used weapons specific to a human/siren for Grace and saved the elephant gun for me. Father had managed to get the doctor to tell us what he knew about the poison. That mix of poison and iron would have slowed me down but only temporarily. Maybe they planned to capture me? But then why bother attacking Grace?

Unless they were sending a message.

If so, the illiterates should have used e-mail.

Were they really after Grace? I suppose someone who didn't understand her unique biology might have thought their hodge-podge of a potion would work. It almost had. Could still.

Don't think about that right now. Concentrate.

That meant someone knew we were on the case, but how likely was that? That, or someone recognized her and took a shot, which was even less likely.

It could have been random anti-Faerie violence, I supposed. Some punks with a tranquilizer gun and their own special formula out hunting centaurs like an evil Elmer Fudd—huhuhuh, be vewwy qwiet. I'm hunting fairwy. Or maybe they were hoping to take out a nymph who was plying a trade she'd have never needed to take if she hadn't followed the lure of adventure in this new Mundane world.

It didn't matter. Even without the disguise, no Mundane would recognize Grace as a Faerie.

Maybe someone protecting a building, not sure what to expect, and had prepared for both Faerie and Mundane intruders?

There was nothing unusual that I could find, no scent of magic to indicate either an arcane attack or Grace defending herself, no suspicious leavings that would suggest a person lying in ambush. Kel said their rookie found Grace in the shadows of the alley, but I couldn't find any evidence that she'd been dragged there. Had she already found her mark and was skulking behind cover, or was she drawn there—and if so, how and by whom?

Kel was right: This was not a good part of town. In fact, since I'd started cleaning up my neighborhood, now dubbed "Territory," a lot of the less desirable elements who preferred to deal with the police than a dragon had migrated here. Still, nothing in the immediate buildings stood out. There was a dry cleaner, a restaurant, and a thrift store, intermixed with townhomes that had seen better days. The lights were out in the townhomes. I'd have to come back tomorrow to see if I could find the anonymous caller who reported the scream.

I flew down to the alley, scaring off the usual complement of vermin and strays. Whatever had happened here hadn't been high-powered or un-familiar enough to scare away the locals. I sniffed around, discovering the usual unpleasant mix of rotting food, trash, excrement. It had been hours since Grace had been discovered; the human smells all mingled and interfered with each other. I could make out Kel's. Another near his was prob-ably the rookie's. But there were dozens more, any of them could be from the EMTs or the trash men who came each morning. There was even evidence of a nymph prostitute earning a few days' rent. I'd need to know what I was sniffing for to recognize anyone.

Besides, a good tranquilizer gun could shoot from up to 45 meters. I'd bet given Grace's injuries that they were closer, but that still put them out among an even greater mix of smells. The roofs were mostly devoid of recent scents, except for the restaurant, which had a rooftop bar.

There was the usual graffiti on the walls, including the swastika "stamped" over a sketch of the Mundane-accepted symbol for Faerie, a black oak. It looked like it'd been there a while. I fought the urge to rake my claws over it.

Dragons were territorial by nature, and I'd claimed Los Lagos as my overall territory for as far as I could fly in a morning and certain areas inside that in particular. It was something the Faerie, human and Magical, understood, and for the most part, respected. Even when they tried to operate above, below, or around the laws of God and Man, they were always aware they risked the chance of dealing with me. Mundanes, however, were slower on the pick-up.

I wondered what it was going to take to explain it to them, and how much it would cost me with God. Just as every good deed earned me back a fraction of my former dragon glory, every sin was paid with remission. Eating sapient beings was a sin.

Of more immediate concern, of course, was the local police. While my neighbors in Territory appreciated and even requested my mark, Captain Santry had made it clear he considered it vandalism. Even in Territory, I sometimes get threatened with fines, and he'd made it clear that he had a nice straw-lined cell waiting for me if I started raking my claws elsewhere.

I decided to risk it. The bricks made deep, dull screeches as my claws raked across the red-painted symbol of hate. Maybe some of them could take a hint.

Then again, maybe they would think Wolverine was on vacation from the Xavier Institute.

There wasn't anything more to be gained from hanging around, so I took to the air. There was a nearby park with a pond I could rinse off in, then I'd head to Eva's hotel. I hadn't trusted her from the start, and now I was ready to get some answers or some revenge.

The Inn at Los Lagos was in the city center, an aging four-story affair that towered over the buildings in its immediate area yet was dwarfed by the newer office buildings just a few blocks away. Still, the economic boom that the opening of the Gap had brought to Los Lagos had saved it from disappearing into obscurity, and its new stucco job attested to some major renovations while the overbearing neon billboard in front declared its pleasure in welcoming both Faerie and Mundanes to the Comparative Artifacts Conference.

Despite their advertised open-mindedness, this was not an area I usually frequented. Tonight of all nights, I didn't want to risk sending any night desk clerk screaming for his mommy or calling the police, so I invited myself to Eva's balcony on the third floor. I landed with a lightness of foot that most Mundanes are surprised to find in a dragon and tapped on her sliding glass door with one claw until I heard movement from within. Then I tapped a little more until I heard the footfalls heading my way.

Eva pulled back the vertical blinds, gave a little shriek to see my face only inches from the plate glass, and hastened to unlock the door and pull it open. She stepped out quickly, pulling her silk robe a little more tightly around her against the cool early morning air. Her face was washed clean of makeup, though she still had the contacts in, and her hair wasn't too badly rumpled. She didn't look like she'd been asleep, and not like she'd been making a restless attempt at it, either.

She regarded me with confusion for a moment, but whether in surprise or because she wasn't sure how to address me, or both, I couldn't tell. Finally, she stammered, "I was watching the television. I saw about the fire. They said a man died."

"A nymph as well." I knew. I had carried the scent of their deaths in the soot on my scales. I'd been making myself not think about it. "That's not why I'm here."

"Of course. I wasn't expecting you until the morning—I mean later this morning. Is something wrong? My brother?"

"We never found your brother. My partner has been shot."

"Oh, my God," she swayed a little and looked for a seat to collapse in, but when none offered itself, she swallowed hard instead and invited me in.

She'd rented herself a comfortable little suite, done in a fair replica of Duke Galen's guest rooms, but on a much smaller scale. She hadn't unpacked her suitcase, although I caught the glimpse of a dress through the crack in the closet door. Red, some kind of rayon/silk blend I'd bet, cut low in the neckline and high in the hem. Probably the one she wore to the bar. I'm sure if I asked her about it, she'd concoct an excuse about trying to be convincing. Frankly, I didn't care.

Eva walked restlessly to the nightstand and pulled out the chair, but didn't sit in it. "What happened?" she asked as she watched her own fingers tap a nervous staccato on its carved lacquered wood.

"That's what I need to know. Tell me everything that happened this evening."

"Well, I, I met that man at the lobby. I think Sister Grace was there, but I couldn't be sure. I think it was her—brown hair, wearing a bulky fisherman's sweater over dark slacks? She was good. I never saw her look our way. She seemed to be reading and texting on her phone."

I nodded, and she began to pace as she continued. "We went into the bar. I didn't really look for Sister Grace, like I'd promised. I just happened to notice her as I looked around the room. There were a couple of other patrons there. I guess there's some kind of conference in the area. Anyway, my 'contact' bought me a drink I didn't have much of. I tried to pay him off, but he didn't want my money. I refused to take things further until he took me to my brother, but I gave him enough to keep him interested—"

"Right there in the bar?"

Suddenly, she stopped her rambling explanation and met my gaze straight on. "Listen, I don't know how you dragons do it—"

"We don't."

"Then you'll have to take my word for it. There are ways to be discreet and yet keep things...interesting." For a moment, she smiled, sly and proud, then seemed to remember herself and shuddered.

I nodded. I'd seen enough human flirtations to know she spoke truthfully. Interesting that she was proud of her performance, though, given how worried she claimed to be about her brother. I filed that away for later. "Go on."

She began to pace again. "He took a message from me for my brother and said he'd call me tomorrow. He said that if nothing else, Weylin might be able to write back."

"What'd the note say?"

"Just a plea to come home, an apology for whatever I'd done, I don't remember exactly. He'd brought paper with him, and I wrote it at the bar."

That checked out with Grace's comment about her writing something. "Which way did he go after he left the hotel?"

"I don't know. We said goodbye at the bar."

"What about his partner?"

"His partner?" She gave a guilty start, then her eyes widened in horror and her hands flew to her face. "You think he had someone working with him? Someone who noticed Grace following him and shot her? Will he come after me next?"

Her fear was genuine, but it didn't explain her first reaction. She'd known he wasn't working alone. I sat back on my haunches, curled my tail around me, and stretched, extending my front claws. Very catlike, but far more menacing.

"I think my partner is in serious danger and you are, too, but if you don't start playing straight with me it'll be a toss-up where the greater danger is. My nun is in the hospital because you weren't honest with us. I'm not in the mood for games."

She paled and sat down hard on the edge of the rumpled bed. "You're scaring me."

Good. "Then you'd better give me the real story, so I can decide if you're a client or not. As a rule, I don't eat clients." I gave her my reassuring half grin, and she relaxed a smidge. I'd been practicing this Good-Cop/Bad-Cop shtick long enough I could do it all on my own.

She toyed with the tie of her robe. "All right. Weylin is in trouble, but it's not with a cult. He has something—something that doesn't belong to him. Its owners are dangerous people. They'll kill him! I begged them to give me a chance to make things right, to convince him to return it himself—"

"So what were you writing?"

She pulled at the tie of her robe. "A...promissory note. A secret about myself that he could use as collateral if I don't come through. I could be in real trouble, Vern. I have to find Weylin and convince him to get it back. You don't understand what's at stake!"

I held up a claw to forestall her yammering. My partner was in a hospital fighting for her life. I couldn't care less what trouble her secret could get her into. "What did Weylin steal?"

"It's not like that! It's an artifact. It's supposed to have great power, and he knew in their hands..."

I don't have eyebrows I can raise, but I can do a fair approximation with a head tilt. She stopped with an apology and took a breath before starting again more coherently.

"The artifact. It's a spear of some kind. They say it's magical—"

"Faerie?" There were strict laws about trafficking magical items. My universe had plenty of artifacts powerful enough to blow a hole in both our worlds. There were restrictions in place to prevent their being imported into the Mundane, but that didn't mean things didn't find their way, regardless. In fact, Grace and I had met over a piece of Faerie music that had summoned a monster from hell to the Mundane, and that was child's play.

I suppressed a groan. Not another Save The Universes Case.

Fortunately, she shook her head. "No, I don't think so. No. They've definitely had it since before the Gap, but now, people are so much more willing to believe in magic, and I think they'd planned to get a mage or someone to, I don't know, activate it? Is that possible?"

I gave a noncommittal grunt. Mages could endow Mundane articles with limited power—like Grace's guardian angel medallion—but to activate a Mundane artifact with powers that legends said it already possessed? I really, really didn't want to find out.

"Then I can't give it to them," she whispered, then buried her head in her hands. "Oh, Detective Vern, you have to help me! We have to find my brother and that artifact. Maybe—I don't know—you could help us escape to Faerie, find someone to destroy it?"

Right. Let the wildcard client and her wayward brother take a potentially dangerous artifact across the Gap? Did she think I was that stupid or that her big brown eyes would have an effect on me?

I wanted to laugh in her face, but that would not help my case—or Grace. I took a breath. "One thing at a time. Who're 'they'?"

"I'm not sure. I mean, they don't have a name. They operate behind the scenes, pulling strings, but when bad things happen—big, bad things— they're involved somehow."

How ominous and unhelpful. "The Illuminati, really? What 'big, bad' things? Terrorism? International crime? The WWE? Hollywood divorces?"

She crooked a smile and wiped her eyes with the edge of her index finger, careful of her immaculately painted nail. "All of that, and worse. I think they want to engineer Armageddon, that's how twisted they are."

Armageddon. Yep, another STUC. "My rates just went up."

She blinked at me, but when I didn't smile to indicate a joke, she got her purse. As she fed bills into my hand, she protested, "But they shot your partner! What about revenge?"

"'Vengeance is mine, sayeth the Lord,'" I quoted as I gathered the greenbacks. "Me, I've got bills to pay."

I clutched the money in my claws. I'd tuck them away later. Dragons had a special pouch under their chests for holding treasures. Now it held my cell phone, lock picks, and apparently, blood money.

I was a dragon. I didn't have a problem with blood—or even treasure earned by blood. But this was different. This was Grace's blood.

Chapter Four:
Junior and the Fat Man

I asked Eva a few more questions, got a few more marginally helpful answers, and told her to lock her doors after I'd gone. Then I perched on the roof while I decided my next move.

Just like the people of Los Lagos, Summer and Fall were in a fight over who had the right to be there. The air had that early morning chill that promised that the day would start out cool, then turn into a scorcher by mid-afternoon. Sounded good to me. Faerie dragons don't age, and magic kept us at a relatively even body temperature, but that doesn't mean we can't get an ache in our wings when the weather's cold. Besides, I hadn't slept or eaten in a continually active 24 hours, and that made me feel everything all the more.

This early, my main source of local research was closed. The Colt's Hoof, the nearby dive for Faerie and Mundanes operating on both sides of the law and the shady areas in between, didn't start hopping until Happy Hour, and if any of my sources from there were still out, they were probably making trouble for the waitresses at Denny's.

That's what I told myself. Truth was, I didn't feel up to dealing with anyone's questions about Grace when I didn't have answers. Seeing her so still on that bed, those tubes coming out of her, the machines beeping to a cadence that wasn't quite right for her...

I decided to walk home, following Grace's route to the hotel. Maybe I'd catch a clue along the way. Besides, I was tired.

So tired, in fact, that it was a couple of blocks before I realized I had a tail that had nothing to do with my anatomy.

I sighed. Did I miss any clues along with missing my stalker? I needed a nap. Still, first things first.

I didn't vary my path. I wanted to get to my own familiar turf before I dealt with this guy. I did, however, pay a little more attention to my senses. I couldn't help Grace if I got ambushed too.

Junior Detective Boy was flying solo. What breeze there was blew in my direction, bearing the scent of Brute which was what had alerted me to him in the first place. He was actually rather good at stalking, so that mistake meant he was skilled but stupid or just plain arrogant. I could work with either.

I could detect dry-cleaning chemicals under the cologne, so the guy either wasn't hurting for money or was hoping he'd look like an early-morning businessman on the way to work. Fat chance. Mundanes love their cars too much. I picked up the scent of cold steel—or more accurately, warm steel. His hand must have been gripping the gun the entire time. From what I could tell by listening to the movement of fabric as he ducked into an alleyway to keep out of sight, he had on a light jacket at most, so he couldn't be hiding the elephant gun. I felt reassured. Conventional bullets hurt, but I could handle them.

We were coming to a nice little maze of alleys I was familiar with. Thanks to renovations in the area, it looked like a regular-sized backway to start, but two newer, larger buildings quickly cut down both space and visibility. I took a left, upped my pace, then used my inherent magic and

Grace's charm to silently rise about ten feet and faded into the shadows.

Junior entered cautiously, then upped his pace when he didn't see me. As soon as he was under me, I swooped down, snagged his shoulders with my back claws, and took off. He gave a kind of girly shriek—not unlike a number of knights I'd tried this trick on in the past. It was so much more satisfying now than it had been during the fire. It took me back to the good ol' days.

He struggled until he realized how far he'd fall if I dropped him, after which he hung on for dear life. I took the opportunity to pick his pockets with my tail.

"Good morning!" I said cheerfully.

"Let me down!"

"Oh, you want down?" I relaxed one set of claws slightly. Again the girlie shriek. Sounded like the cry room at church. "Tell you what: You answer my very important questions, and I'll let you down the right way. Give me any heartburn, and I'll let you down the easy way. Believe me—it won't take much to get on my nerves. I've had a very bad day. Now, who're you working for?"

"I don't know what you're talking about. Help!" He wrapped his arms around my calf.

O.K. Skilled and stupid it was. I pumped my wings, and we rose. "They say in space, no one can hear you scream. Shall we test that theory?"

His shouting died into a gurgle, and he started pleading—with God, not me. Typical human, always going straight to the top. "God helps those who help themselves," I quipped at him. "Tell me who set you on my tail. And talk fast. My tail's getting tired."

"I work for Mr. Ramada—Cambridge Ramada!"

"You're kidding me." His parents must've been friends with Paris Hilton's. "What's Cambridge want with me?"

"Not you—the artifact! He wants the artifact. Oh, God, please let me down! I swear I'll take you to him and he can explain everything!"

"I'll let you down when we get to Cambridge."

"Where?"

Under other circumstances, I might have been tempted to play out the comedy with Cambridge's name. However, I had too much else on my mind and the nagging feeling that I was operating on an increasingly shrinking deadline. Besides, I'd carried so many people today, my claws were sore. I didn't know how long I could hang onto this loser, and cliché and threats aside, I didn't want to drop him to his doom.

I hollered, "Your boss, Cambridge! Tell me where he's staying, and we'll take care of this right now."

Cambridge Ramada had eschewed his namesake for the Broadmoor Los Lagos, a luxury hotel built to accommodate all the Faerie nobility and Mundane upper crust that had business here on the edge of the Gap. Nestled in the mountainside like its sister hotel in Colorado Springs, it was as far above Eva's caliber as her digs were from mine.

Nonetheless, when I landed at the *porte cochere* outside the lobby and released Junior, the doorman didn't even blink, just opened a door and greeted us with a friendly "Welcome to the Broadmoor, sirs." That's class.

The sedate atmosphere rubbed off on Junior, apparently. As soon as I released him from my claws, he caught his balance, straightened his jacket and dusted off his pants, and sauntered in. It was almost like he hadn't been screaming like a ninny for the past three miles. I followed, winking at the doorman as I passed.

The elevator was large enough to accommodate me—class again—so we made our way to Ramada's room, me with my tail against Junior's back. A companionable gesture at first glance, but in truth, I was pressing the spikes of my tail along the vertebrae of his neck.

Mr. Ramada surprised me by having one of the more modest suites in the hotel, with a long couch and a large, sturdy chair. He needed it, too. I could live for a week on this guy—if my taste buds could handle that much blubber. He was either an early riser or Junior had called him before he started tailing me, because he met us dressed in a casual outfit that was obviously tailored to compliment his girth. Maybe he'd planned to take Junior to the Country Club after he was done with me.

"Well," he said, not bothering to rise from his comfy chair, "this is not quite what we'd had in mind."

"Next time, send somebody less hygienic," I replied. "You should pour that bottle of Brute down the sink."

"Yes, why don't you do that while the dragon and I talk?" Ramada waved toward one of the bedrooms, and like a sulky teenager, Junior disappeared into it. "I'd offer you a seat, Mister...?"

"Vern will do. What I really want are answers. Why'd you send Junior Detective Boy after me?"

"Junior Detective Boy," Ramada chuckled like he was trying to force it out of his throat and the roof of his mouth simultaneously. Maybe he was trying to sound like Sydney Greenstreet playing Casper Gutman, but it came out like an asthmatic Beavis and Butthead.

"I hope you're not going to tell me you're looking for a black bird," I said.

Again the laugh. "No, nor will I say Peters is like a son to me. May I assume you're suspicious enough of your client? She did not steal something from me, though it is true we are both after the same object. You are familiar with the Lance of Longinus?"

"I've had some experience with the Faerie version." Inside, I groaned. The lance was the one used by the Roman soldier Longinus to pierce the side of Christ. As such it was endowed with supernatural power, but since the stabbing occurred after Jesus's death and before his Resurrection—i.e., the three days he spent in Hell redeeming those damned who would listen—the nature of its power remained indeterminate.

Longinus did become Christian, but he also continued his career as a soldier, rising in ranks until he commanded his own centuria. Thus, the power molded itself to his personality. Anyone wielding the Lance of Longinus had the power to command the unresisting obedience of anyone under them, yet also stayed obedient to whomever they recognized as their leader. In Longinus's case, all hundred of his men followed him to martyrdom.

It had disappeared after that, probably falling into the hands of people who didn't know what they had, until it resurfaced in the Patisserie Wars. That was before my time working with the Church, but I'm told the violence that ensued over tranche cakes nearly tore Europe apart. When Pope Paul XI intervened and brought peace, Vatican control of the lance was part of the package. There it remained under lock and wards until a misguided monk seduced by a Fallen Angel took it upon himself to use the lance to bring good to the world.

There's a reason Jesus refused Satan's offer to rule the Earth.

That was over a century ago—our Great War. Some of the darkest years in Faerie history. I was on the Inquisition then, assigned to find the lance and destroy it. When I did, its power backlashed on me. It took me years to recover physically, decades psychologically, which was why I had been pulling a plow for the Silent Brothers of St. Osgood when the Gap opened, and I found myself Called to this world.

Still, the lance had been destroyed, and I told Cambridge so.

"Hehmmn, hehmnn. So my research has shown, though I have not been able to obtain the details. Perhaps when this is over, we could discuss it over a long lunch? What I am concerned about right now is the Mundane Lance of Longinus.

"You see, I too, am an investigator of sorts, and my current client is a collector of antiquities with fascinating histories. Now you may be aware that there are several theories concerning the whereabouts of the fabled Lance of Longinus? One holds that it is in the Shatzkammer in Vienna, but another asserts that that one is a copy commissioned by Himmler for display in Nuremberg while the original was used for secret occult ceremonies." Again, the laugh. "Intriguing, isn't it? So then, the tale goes that the true spear was actually sent to Antarctica, to be buried with the ashes of Hitler and his beloved Eva."

"Eva?"

"Yes. Marvelous coincidence, is it not? Of course, such a prize could not remain forever—hehmm, hehmmn—on ice, so it was supposedly unearthed by one Colonel Maximillian Hartman, who is at large in Europe. Current conspiracy theorists say it played a part in 9-11. My investigations indicate certain parties have it here in Los Lagos, with the intention of carrying it across the Gap to see if it can be endowed with a spell to enhance any powers it may have."

"If that's true, my rates just went up."

"As have mine. We are not so dissimilar, I think. My client wants the lance-at-Large for his private collection, and I do not think he either believes in its powers or would take advantage of such powers even if they were real. Otherwise, I would not have taken him as a client. I, too, have my own sense of morality, you see."

Morality? I had to question the morality of someone who would send an armed man after a dragon. At least, one that didn't have a grudge against him. "I follow God's morality."

"Yes, of course." He nodded, and I genuinely believed he understood all that implied. He changed the subject. "It had been my intention to have you followed while I continued my own investigations. Now, however, perhaps we could work together?"

"I have a client."

He cocked a brow at me skeptically. "And are you certain of her intentions? I have not concerned myself overmuch with her, yet I've found it curious how often I've encountered her in association with the lance these past months. Well, let me propose this: Should you find the lance before I, at least give me the opportunity to present my client's case and bona fides. My client is more than capable of refunding Miss Heidler's fee and compensating you for your troubles."

I had to admit, the promise of pay, along with a chance to vet the client, appealed to me. I didn't trust Eva, especially since all the evidence led to someone knowing ahead of time about Grace, and the only person with that knowledge should have been her.

Cambridge took my hesitation as agreement. "So, partners?"

That was the wrong thing to ask. I remembered now why I'd come here. "My partner is in the hospital, hanging onto life by her fingernails because of a poison dart meant for me. You know anything about that?"

He looked surprised, enough that I believed he had nothing to do with it. "I assure you, my style is not to accost fellow colleagues—particularly when their work furthers mine. However..." He paused, tapping his teeth with a well-manicured nail. I waited until he pursed his lips, satisfied at whatever idea he'd had, and continued.

"Perhaps I can sweeten the deal. Help me, and I'll make sure my client gets your partner the best medical care money can buy—Faerie or Mundane. And in the meantime, I shall add the search for the antidote, should there be one, to my own investigations. Your partner is female?"

"Faerie woman, human/siren."

He shook his head, his jovial demeanor gone. "Such a pity. This is a difficult business for women."

"She can hold her own," I said, yet my words sounded hollow and false to my own ears.

Chapter Five: The Fall Drake

Cambridge had Junior—I'd never be able to call him by the same name as the Father of the Church—escort me to the lobby, which he did with a scowl that was half-menace, half-sulk. I was too tired even to come up with a smart-aleck comment. There were a hundred things I needed to do, but thanks to my unexpected flight carrying Junior, a nap was top of the list. My wings ached too much to fly, and I was too tired to walk, so I had the concierge call a Rhyde and put it on Ramada's tab. It was his fault I was so far from home, anyway.

They offered the options of open-bed trucks and horse trailers now to accommodate their larger Faerie clientele. I could fit in an SUV or a minivan with the seats out, but I asked for a truck. With my luck, the SUV would be an econobox model, and I didn't feel like trying to crowd into the back. I also didn't want to smell horse for the next half-hour by taking a trailer. The ashes were bad enough. Besides, the air was cool but not cold. Maybe I'd wake up some. I had the driver take me to the hospital.

Slipping into Grace's room was a lot easier this time. No one paid any attention as I boarded the elevator, slunk past the ICU nurse, and entered. That did not fill me with confidence. Neither did the fact that no one had checked on her since about an hour after I'd left. Mundanes, always letting their machines do the work for them. Grace needed someone at her side, praying for her, telling her to hang on, promising everything would be okay.

I couldn't promise that—to her or to myself. I couldn't even pray. I was so angry and tired. Walking into this room full of cold tech and devoid of warm feelings, I felt the weight of my worries smothering me like the ashes of the fire.

"You'd probably tell me I wasn't being fair, that Mundane medicine helped you when all the prayers and well wishes and even magic could not," I said to her still form. "You'd probably remind me that we use technology, too. So wake up and say it, already. Please, Grace. Wake up?"

My only reply was the rhythmic hiss of her ventilator.

I settled my chin on her stomach, then placed her hand on my head, just behind the horns. She couldn't caress me, but somehow, I just needed that contact.

I slouched there, drifting between angry thoughts about Mundanes and dozing half-dreams about the times when Faeries tried to kill me, when the sound of the door opening caught me by surprise. My eyes sprung open, and I growled.

A guy in blue scrubs gaped at me, then spun and ran off. Great. What do I do now?

A moment later, the nurse from Little Flower popped in, the med tech in tow.

"Oh, Vern. When did you get here?"

I appreciated that she didn't ask "how" almost as much as I appreciated her tone, as if I had every right to be in this room. Because of that, I felt myself replying honestly.

"I needed to check on her, to let her know..." I stopped, embarrassed. Let Grace know what?

That this case had become a tangled mess, that I was no closer to finding our missing brother, much less a cure for her? That all of it had to do with a Mundane artifact whose counterpart had started our Great War?

I hadn't told Grace any of that. I hadn't even told her to hang on.

"Well, she's stable right now," the nurse said, checking some readings and noting them in Grace's chart. "Doctor Sidwell has contacted Grace's mother superior, and they are arranging to be here later today. We're doing everything we can for her."

"Really?" I could not help the sardonic tone in my voice.

Somehow, however, she understood my intent. "I pray the rosary at the nurse's station for all our patients. Why don't you go home and get some sleep? I'll call you if anything changes."

It was a nicer dismissal than she gave the police officer earlier, but it was a dismissal, nonetheless. I thanked her, apologized to her assistant for growling at him, and went home.

Without Cambridge to bankroll my ride this time, I flew home, then stumbled into my lair, sure I'd sleep as soon as I hit my pad.

The place was almost eerie in its quiet. I've lived alone most of my existence, and I hadn't realized how used I'd gotten to hearing Grace's breathing coming from her upstairs bedroom. Then I called in the dogs, and they snuggled up against me for a nap.

I hadn't been asleep more than an hour when a loud, authoritative knock awakened me. The dogs sprang alert, barking and bouncing. I growled at them, and they fell silent. I could make dogs understand who was alpha in my house—or anywhere else.

I hadn't bothered to lock the door. Maybe I'd been too tired. Maybe I was subconsciously spoiling for a fight. Regardless, I was awake and annoyed, but calm. Good thing, too, because after a second run of three sharp raps, my visitors entered. Captain Michael Santry, chief of police for Los Lagos, ignored the dogs bounding at his heels and strode past the office to my living quarters, followed closely by a weary Kel. I settled myself like a cat on a windowsill, my forearms crossed before me. I was too tired for anthropomorphiza-tion, and besides, I knew it annoyed Santry.

"Where were you last night?" he demanded as soon as he cleared the door. He saved his manners for when Grace was around.

"Good morning to you, too. I was asleep—at least until you woke me."

"Before that?"

"At the hospital. Grace was shot—"

"I know that! I also know you only stuck around for about half an hour after Officer Killian here left. Where did you go then?"

"I had business. Detective business. Then I went back to the hospital and came home."

"Could you be more specific?"

I really hated getting the third degree in my own home. "Not without risking client confidenti-ality—or without a compelling reason." Santry sneered at this. "I can tell you I'm looking for Grace's attacker."

His manner didn't soften as much as I'd ex-pected. Grace and he had formed a rapport from the day they'd met. He's been her ally when the rest of the town was against her, even standing strong against the city council when they were screaming for her arrest.

Something was going on—something he thought involved me and not her.

Even so, he did ask, "Any success?"

I wanted to be mollified, but his concern was too little, too late. Not to mention, I felt like there was more to his question than the two words he spoke.

"Some," I answered.

Santry waited, but when I didn't elaborate, he tried a different tactic. "We'd like to look around the place."

I yawned and stretched, extending my claws, then settled back into my original position. "Fine. Come back later with the search warrant and a crew of about twelve. It's a big place. Think you could ask them to sweep as long as they're finger-print dusting?"

"Don't get smart with me—"

"Can't help it. Says so on my website: 'Wisdom of the ages, knowledge of eternity. Virginity confirmed.' Though that doesn't mean as much to you Mundanes—"

"Cut the crap!"

"Then tell me what this is about." I forced my-self to keep my voice even.

"What this is about? Your partner is barely alive, and I've got two new murders on my hands! I want answers. Now tell me where you were last night—in detail—or we can take this downtown."

"Murders?"

"Don't play stupid. One has 'dragon attack' written all over it. You want to come quietly?"

Dragon attack? I busted out laughing. Just when I thought things couldn't get more compli-cated. Never mind that I'd just saved a half-dozen or more people from a fire that some anti-Faerie type probably started. Never mind all the times I'd saved this world from itself. No, now someone got stupidly dead, and they wanted to blame me?

"Santry, did you get less sleep than me? How would you even know what a dragon attack looks like? Did Vialpando make that determination? Because Kel's smarter than that." Vialpando was Santry's best friend, a detective on the force who liked me about as much as Santry and didn't bother to hide it under a veneer of politeness, no matter how thin.

Kel pleaded with his eyes, but whether it was for me to not involve him or to cooperate, I didn't know.

Santry's patience for me was even less than his usual from our pre-Grace years. "Fine. Let's discuss this at the precinct."

"You got a warrant?"

Now, he laughed. "Who's being stupid now? I don't need a warrant. You're not a person in my government's eyes and you know it. I can bring you in for questioning any time I want. I know the law, especially when it comes to you. I don't even have to arrest you. I can just impound you like an animal—"

"Lancelot's sword, you will! I already spent my time in your precious city zoo, and you're not taking me back." I was so done with Mundanes lording over me. I reared up, wings unfurled, cheek crests flared, every inch the wild dragon.

"I'm busy, Santry, and I'm not in the mood for your games."

Santry crossed his arms. "Neither am I."

I've never yet met a knight that had anything on a burned-out copper with a distrust for magic and a grudge against private investigators. Santry met me glare for glare.

Kel stepped in between us. "Come on, Vern, you know how this works. We gotta follow leads, even if they're wrong. Look, we just need to know where you were tonight. Help us narrow this down."

I settled back into my original position, and Santry backed off. "I left the hospital and checked the alley where you'd found Grace. I didn't find anything of value, so I went looking for other clues. I've been all around this town tonight. Even the Broadmoor. Don't ask why. Client confidentiality. Otherwise, I was keeping a low profile. You should know that, Kel. You were the one that told me about the poison dart, never mind all the anti-Faerie sentiment in the air right now. When I didn't find anything useful, I went back to the hospital to check on Grace, then came here to catch a nap before I started my investigations again.

"I was not checking my phone, so I can't give you times. The doorman at the Ramada can probably tell you when I entered and exited, and the ICU nurse about when I was in the hospital. No one saw me go in, though, and I don't know how long I was there. Satisfied?"

He didn't seem especially so. "Can you narrow down when you were at the crime scene?"

"Why? Come on, Santry. You can't think I actually attacked someone, tonight of all nights?"

"Someone's shot your partner. Started a fire in your so-called territory. Lot of hate on the streets right now."

"Lot of hate in here," I retorted.

Kel clenched his fists and looked at us both in askance. "Just help us narrow this down. It's in your best interest, too."

I gave him a break. He looked like he'd had a worse night than I had. With a heavy sigh, I gave him the times as best I could remember.

"And no one was there?" Kel asked.

"No, and nothing out of the ordinary."

"What about the swastika that was scratched through?"

I rolled my eyes. "Really? I thought you said this was about a couple of murders, not some petty so-called vandalism. Alleged vandalism."

"Were you trying to send a message?" Santry asked.

Not only was I taken aback by his insight, but I was nagged by the conviction that I was missing something. I answered carefully. "My mark always carries a message, not that you Mundanes ever get it."

"Did you think the blood would make it clearer, then?"

"What blood? I didn't find any blood on the scene—other than a trace of Grace's that is. Trust me; I'd still be following that trail if I had."

"Maybe you did," Santry snarled at me.

"What?"

Again, Kel stepped in with the explanation. I had a vision of him and Santry in the car, deciding who would play Good Cop, not that there was any doubt. "We found blood in the scratches."

I snorted. Someone was embellishing my mark now? I really hated this day. "Well, it wasn't mine."

"Of course not," Santry snapped. "It belonged to the dead man we found in the alley three hours ago."

"What?"

Santry pulled out his phone and showed me a photo of my mark, bearing dried drips of blood.

Then he swiped to the next photo. The man Grace had been following lay in a mangled pile behind a dumpster. One arm had been torn off, like hacked and yanked out of its socket, and he bore several deep, wide puncture marks. Parts of his flesh looked ripped; I could see bone. No wonder Santry suspected me. I closed my eyes and prayed for patience.

"So he looks familiar?" I could hear the smirk in Santry's voice.

He was talking about the attack, of course, but I said, "That's the guy Grace was tailing."

"We figured as much. We found a dart matching the one that struck Sister Grace in his pocket. Now, are you ready to come to the station and discuss it, maybe with a lawyer present?"

My eyes flew open, and I gaped at him. "You cannot be serious! Why don't you talk to the coroner first—or maybe a vet? First off, if I'm going to kill something, I'm going to eat it, no matter how distasteful."

"Unless you were sending a message," Santry countered.

"Then I'd have just left the head—and in the case of you Mundanes, some words, since your skulls are thick and your brains tiny. But seriously? You think I'd implicate myself so obviously? How would that help me or Grace?

"Further, these teeth—" I indicated my canines. "—are for piercing and holding prey. If I want to bite through bone, I use the front ones. Don't believe me? Ask a vet, or maybe a paleontologist. Finally, if I thought this guy poisoned Grace, do you think I'd kill him without getting the antidote? Because that's my priority. I'll leave the vengeance to God."

He didn't buy that line like Eva had. "Would you? Maybe he did give you the antidote. Maybe it's being made right now."

"In which case, I'd be at Grace's side, telling her to hold on. Instead, I've been flying around all night grasping at any tenuous leads I could find and coming up with nothing. I came home—because, like you, I've been trying to track down a killer. Unlike you, I didn't have a night of sleep beforehand. If I'm going to be any help to Grace, I need to be sharp. I came home for a short nap until I could start checking out my leads."

"What leads do you have?"

I growled. Why did everyone want me to do their work for them? "Nothing conclusive. And nothing I can share without putting my client—or Grace—in further danger."

"I could bring you in." I wasn't sure if Santry meant it as an offer or a threat, but at least his tone and stance had both become more reasonable. For that matter, I had to wonder how much he really thought I was the murderer. I didn't sense any backup waiting outside in case I got violent.

I decided to try reason. "Santry, we are dealing with things that go beyond the Mundane. I need to be free to work in my own way. I'll get to the bottom of this, believe me."

"And when you do, you'll bring him to me instead of dealing with him yourself?" Santry asked.

I shrugged. "Sure. We can even do the Good Cop/Bad Cop shtick."

At my joke, Kel broke into a grin that was half relief.

Santry, however, sighed. "It's not a shtick. Two people are dead, and one I happen to admire greatly is just hanging on. If you have any information that can put that murderer behind bars, I want it—but, do what you have to do."

"So don't eat anyone until we have a chance to question him," Kel added, trying to lighten the mood. Santry glared at him. He never has appreciated that kind of humor.

I escorted them out. As we passed the kitchen area, Santry noticed Junior's gun, which I'd carelessly tossed on the table on my way in. "What's this?"

"Found it last night. I was going to destroy it as soon as I got up."

"You should have turned it in to us right away. It could have been used in a crime."

I was feeling generous. Besides, Grace had told me to be nicer to Santry. "Tell you what. Dust it for prints and run a ballistics check. If it's evidence, it's yours. Otherwise, I get to flame it."

"There's always more where it came from."

"If you can't beat them, inconvenience them."

I picked up the gun with my tail while I told Kel where to find a plastic baggie. The dogs, reassured by the friendlier tones of their superiors, came bounding out of the back lair to get pets from my "guests" before they left.

I thought Santry would say something cliché about not leaving town or having his eye on me, but he just rubbed one dog's floppy ears and turned to go.

"Hey, Santry."

He paused with his hand on the knob. "Yeah?"

"The dart."

"Empty and clean. No fingerprints."

"Sure it wasn't a plant? Seems to me someone's trying to set me up."

Santry pinched the bridge of his nose with his thumb and forefinger. "It's never easy around you, is it?"

"Not for eight hundred years, Santry. Not for eight hundred years."

Chapter Six:
Faerie-Go-Round

Actually, it was over eight hundred and fifty years since St. George—God bless him, the magically overpowered pain in the tail—trapped me in a spell and took away everything that made me a dragon: my size, my wisdom, my magic, my flight, my fire...

I'm sure he had the best of intentions. For whatever reason, God needed a dragon to do—well, I still wasn't sure what, even after all this time. I also didn't know if I was specifically chosen or just the lucky drake to be in the wrong place at the right time. What I did know was that it required one of my kind to be brought low, and George was all too good at that.

Sometimes, I wonder what would have happened if I hadn't been so stubborn and had just given up after the first swipe of George's blessed sword. But no. I was an eighth-day creation, and no uppity knight with shining armor and a pretty horse was going to get the better of me, even if he did have God on his side.

We all know how that turned out. He did have God on his side, and God wanted a dragon for some ineffable purpose that required it—required me—to submit to the authority of the Faerie Church. After I had lost just about everything except my mind (and even then, I had lost access to a good chunk of my knowledge), George brought me to the Vatican and to Pope Pius, who gave me the moniker "Vern the Wyvern" because he couldn't pronounce my real name and thought he was being clever. He told me that if I followed God's will, I would return to my greatness. And so it's been nearly nine centuries of push and pull, give and take as I figured out what God wants with me.

Of late, that seems to be living in the Mundane as a private detective to the particularly desperate. It hasn't been easy, but it has been interesting.

Some days were a little too interesting.

Thanks to Santry's home invasion I wouldn't get back to sleep anytime soon, so I called Bishop Aiden to check on Mother Angela and to make sure he knew to include healers in the party. I didn't trust Mundane medicine to do more than keep Grace alive until they got there. Something was off about that room.

"What do you mean?" Aiden asked.

I hadn't realized I'd spoken aloud. But when I thought back, I could not point to anything. Yes, I believed they were doing everything they could, despite Doc Pessimism's dire prognosis. No, I didn't sense magic at work, necessarily. But, I had to admit, seeing her like that left me feeling so helpless and angry, I hadn't really been paying attention to the surroundings.

"Get some rest—and pray before you enter her room next time. I'll let Mother Angela know your suspicions when I speak with her."

I promised to pray but not to sleep. I didn't think I'd get much sleep until I knew she was awake.

It was still early, so I padded over to the office to do research. One thing I'd learned fast in the PI business was the value of a good computer. I moved Grace's keyboard off the steel plate where my virtual keyboard would shine. I can do very delicate work, even spent a few decades doing copy work with the Jesuits, but dragon claws are hard on plastic.

The Los Lagos Gazette already had an article about the murders. On the homepage was a lovely photo of our suspect, or at least of his stump of arm soaking in a dark pool of blood. One for the scrapbooks. The accompanying article was full of "No Comments," by law enforcement. Wow—even after all his posturing to me about how it was a dragon attack, he didn't say anything to the press. Some days, I could not figure him out.

Still, that didn't stop the reporter from putting in enough innuendo to set my rep back eight and a half centuries regardless of the facts. I glanced at the byline: Kitty McGrue. Figures. I'd saved her life once but ruined her story in the process. She's never forgiven me.

Research was getting me nowhere, at least nowhere good. I went to morning Mass.

Mass was somber without Grace there. It wasn't just the fact of her injuries, either, although it comforted me to know that some people at least cared about her, and about me. Several parishioners went out of their way after the rosary to approach me with words of reassurance. But the

Mass felt emptier without her voice. I hadn't realized how much I'd come to count on her singing, imbued with the power of her siren heritage, to lift me up during the Psalms. I vowed never to take it for granted again.

Naturally, we prayed for Grace in the special intentions, and when Mass was completed, a handful of the regulars offered to stay and pray an extra rosary with me on her behalf. Since Grace had started cantoring the morning Masses, she'd become a favorite of those who attended. Afterward, I spent a few minutes answering questions and listening to speculations. Quite a few were convinced it was the Neo-Nazis, and they were worried.

One of the grandmothers said, "You know there are some of them in Gina's school? They beat up a Faerie human—a Freshman, I think, poor thing—and they gave a black eye to one of Gina's friends who tried to stop him. At Martin Luther King High!"

"I have offered to go to the schools and tell them about the real Nazis, but the district is afraid it could make things worse," Joseph grumbled. His family had fled Germany after their parish priest was arrested and sent to a concentration camp. "Bah! We must speak now, before the day comes when we cannot speak at all."

"It doesn't matter," one of the homeschooled teens said. "Thanks to social media 'nazi' has been used so freely, it doesn't have the same meaning anymore. People use it for everything from racists to Trump supporters. At this point, people roll their eyes at the word. And of course, the real 'sin' is speaking out against anyone's 'truth,' no matter how evil it is."

"You're too young to be so cynical," I told him.

"Like you're not?" he retorted.

I gave a short laugh. "Kid, I've earned it." I was immortal. I'd seen eras come and go. This one would pass, too. The question was, how bad would it get before it did?

I didn't want to think about that right now. I had more immediate concerns.

I said my goodbyes, but Rosa Costa stopped me in the vestibule.

"Verncito, what can we do for you?"

I felt myself melt a little. The Costas was one of the first families I'd met at the church who were actually willing to brave speaking with me. Their oldest had tried to hire me to protect them from the Chicago mob. That was the most work I'd ever done for a couple of Pokémon cards. I had those cards framed on my wall. Of greater value was their friendship. God had taken away many of my powers, but he'd given me other gifts instead, like the Costas.

Like Grace.

"I'm not sure what you can do. I'll be alright once I know Grace is. I'm going to head to the hospital, then start looking again for the meat that did this." "Meat" was what I called someone who didn't deserve the classification of their species. I had other words for whoever did this to Grace, but none were fit for a church or Rosa's ears.

"Then let me give you a ride. I worry about you being in public right now. The papers—"

"Yeah, I saw. I'm surprised more people didn't run out of the church when I showed up."

"We know you. Kitty McGrue is *muy estupida*. I think it's the 'Fellowship of the Fourth Reich,' hurting Grace and trying to make you take the fall."

"You read too many detective novels," I teased tiredly. Still, Rosa had good instincts. Makes sense; she'd been a mafia wife, even if Jerry had just been a low-level fence and not someone in the "family." She'd seen and learned enough to know how the criminal mind worked. I made a note to check on the Reich.

Next, I went to the hospital. I dropped by the florist shop first and used my sniffer to pick out a bouquet of flowers. If Grace wasn't awake to see them, she could at least smell them. I paid the tongue-tied cashier with some of the money I'd gotten from Eva but remembered the price to add to my expense list.

I must have been an amusing sight, a pony-sized dragon carrying flowers in his mouth. At four feet high at the shoulders, I couldn't even command the gravitas befitting the situation. Still, the morning ICU nurse just nodded sympathetically as I passed by her station. I wondered if the night nurse had briefed her, and if they were letting me in despite the doctor's orders.

Grace hadn't moved since I saw her last. I noticed new equipment, however. When was that healer coming?

Not that I was sure they could help. Mundanes tended to think magic was, well, magic. Snap your fingers, say a spell, maybe apply a potion, and Grace would magically come back to perfect health, maybe after a cliché of a seizure to make everyone worry.

Magic, the all-powerful answer to everything.

Except that it wasn't. Omnipotence belonged only to the Creator. And he wasn't sharing with me. Without knowing what was in the poison, the best a healer could do was encourage Grace's body to heal itself, and that would only work if her body wasn't too far gone.

I had to find who did this.

I spoke gently to Grace, telling her what I'd learned, reminding her that everyone was praying for her. I didn't mention the murders or how I was being implicated. What was the point?

Then I wafted the flowers under her nose.

"I got these for you. Spent our good money on it, too, so you may as well open your eyes and appreciate them because we'll be paying for them with extra cases when you get out of here."

Her nostrils didn't even flare at the sweet, spicy scent.

"Hang on, Grace. I'm going to find who did this to you, and I will find the cure."

⚖

Eva was next on my to-do list. As I landed on the balcony, I saw her reading the paper, her mouth curled in something between a smile and a grimace. Her expression changed, however, as soon as I knocked on the door, and she hastened to open it. "Oh, Vern! I was just reading about the deaths!"

"Seemed kind of pleased."

"I hated that man!" she spat. "He deserved what he got. Oh, but it doesn't help us, does it? Have you located the lance? Or my brother?"

Interesting priorities.

⚖

Given the day I was having, it came as no surprise that I'd forgotten to activate the wards when I'd left my lair. Most people would know better than to invade my home, but not this time.

I found the dogs sprawled in a drugged sleep and heard the sounds of things being overturned from within the warehouse. I decided not to bother with subtlety, but I did resist the urge to just burst in with flames going full blast. Not that I'd regret the loss of detritus that I laughingly called "treasure," but the building did have our equipment and a roof. The insurance company didn't cover Acts of Dragon. Besides, I had questions first.

Naturally, I walked straight in to find six adolescent meatheads pointing weapons at me. Even worse, they weren't my meatheads. These guys wore white clown makeup, like that would hide their identities. One held an automatic weapon—yep, a bona fide black-market AK-47, and I thought only Faerie lived their clichés. Pretty sweet for a kid with zits. He should have used the money on a dermatologist.

I didn't stop, just closed the door with my tail while I strolled in slow and placid-like. My visitors had shaved heads, faces painted white with clown paint, and black t-shirts with a swastika in a white circle.

"If you're the housekeeping service, you're fired."

"You stay right there or we gonna fire you!" said one guy from the sidelines as he held his nunchucks at the ready.

What'd he think he would do—whack me on the nose? I turned to the one holding the assault rifle. "Scraping the bottom of the barrel with that one, weren't you?"

AK4Me hefted the rifle a little higher. It was cute that he thought he looked threatening. "He's right. You just stay still while we search the place."

"The place" was a 10,000-square-foot warehouse with offices on the upper floor. Boxes I still hadn't opened lined the walls and made a maze in the second warehouse room. I settled myself on the floor and rested my head on my crossed front legs. "Go ahead. I get half of anything you find."

They stared at me, unbelieving. I smiled back. Mr. Cooperation, that's me.

Finally, Big Gun snarled for the others to get to work. As he turned his back on me, Nunchucks muttered, "I got your half. Don't think I don't." Guess he learned such witty repartee in Hitler Youth Summer Camp. Los Despredatores were more eloquent and had better banter even in a knife fight—plus, they could do it in two languages.

I said something insulting in German, but with a sweet tone. Blank stares met me. Pitiful.

"If you want to play Nazi, you should at least know the language," I said in German. That time, at least, earned me a "shut up!" although I think they just wanted me to stop talking in general.

I watched, listened, and waited. I had no idea what they were looking for. Well, I did know what they were supposed to be looking for, but I got the feeling these guys were the kind who weren't above pocketing an interesting trinket they could give their girlfriends. Too bad I wasn't supposed to talk. I could direct them to a box of costume jewelry that just made me depressed thinking about the real gems I had in Faerie.

Maybe I should have stopped them from trashing the place. I just didn't have the energy. Besides, with eight teenage skinheads wandering ignorantly around, knocking things over, and gradually making their way toward the back of the lair, it was only a matter of time before they took care of things themselves.

"I wouldn't go in there if I were you," I suggested as Nunchucks made a grab for the doorknob to Grace's workshop.

"You gonna stop me?" He turned the knob.

"Nope," I said as I closed my ears and my eyes. Even so, I saw the otherworldly light and heard the harmonious roar of Divine Vengeance followed by Mundane screams.

"The Heavenly Host on the other hand...."

I waited until the screams died down to whimpers before opening my eyes and rising.

Four of the skinheads were unconscious. Three may as well have been; they were curled up in the fetal position, whimpering. Nunchucks was actually crying for his mommy. Big Guns had collapsed to the floor as well, the gun thrown away from him. He was sitting and rocking and making high-pitched keening through the roof of his mouth.

I'd tell Grace to tone down her wards some, except that the effect is directly proportional to the evilness of the intent. Suddenly, I was feeling a little shaky about my earlier entrance.

Knights out of the armor now. I went around, collecting weapons in the office trash can and poking through pockets. I found the usual stuff— driver's licenses, credit cards, petty cash... One kid had a condom; wishful thinking on his part, I knew. Another had a report card. MLK High. Wonder if he was the one beating up Faerie kids? Honor roll grades, too. Of all the years I've battled evil, there were still some things I didn't understand.

As I was returning Big Guns' (aka Rick Matherston's) wallet back into his jacket pocket, he blinked and focused on me.

"What was that?" he rasped.

"Angels, kid." Actually a kind of magical shadow of the real thing, but close enough.

"But I thought angels were..."

"There's a reason why their first words are usually 'Fear not!' whenever they meet a human."

His eyes returned to their unfocused stare. I almost felt sorry for him. Then I noticed the letters FARI SLAR tattooed on his knuckles.

Faerie slayer. I didn't feel so bad after all.

Chapter Seven: Cranking Up the Heat

The next morning saw me back to my same, tired routine. I awoke before the sun to take care of my personal needs out of sight of parishioners and nosy neighbors. Then I listened to daily Mass.

Grace's wards also contained a spell to repair or clean up much of the damage done by a would-be intruder. In fact, there have been times I'd been tempted to set the spell off just to clean up the place. I'd just come in from finishing up the last chores and checking the dogs when Santry again graced me with his presence, Officer Tracy Sterling in tow. For once, I didn't mind a visit from the "heat."

"Where you been?" he demanded.

"Throwing out the trash. They should be conscious in an hour or so."

Santry hissed through his teeth and turned to Sterling. "Go." The uniform swept past me, pulling out her gun as she went. Smart girl knew the neighborhood.

"Something I can do for you, Santry?" I asked before he could start asking me questions. From beside the building, Tracy called out, "There's six of them in here. Uh, gross! Did you have to put them in the dumpster? I'm calling a wagon!"

"Check the other bin, but it sounds like a couple recovered!" I called back.

"Recovered from what?"

I held up my front paws in a bipedal display of innocence. Looks like his good relationship with Grace was going to work in my favor today. "Grace's security system. I came home to find eight FFR-types searching the place. The Fellowship of the Fourth Reich? One of them made the mistake of trying to open her workroom."

Santry looked like he could use a stiff drink. "Are they going to be all right?"

I shrugged. "Nothing that counseling—and if they're so inclined, absolution—wouldn't fix. So what can I do for you?"

Santry pulled out Junior's gun and passed it to me. I ringed the trigger guard with my claw. "It's clean and unregistered. Think it belonged to your yahoos?"

"Nah, not their style." I headed into my office with Santry following. He gasped when he saw the felonious pile on my desk. "This is what the well-dressed Skinhead is wearing these days."

Santry sighed as he used a pencil to push a switchblade off the automatic weapon. "What'd they want with you, Vern?" He seemed more exasperated than concerned. It almost hurt.

"No idea. Grace's 'Karma shield' got to them before I found out. I found this on one of them, though." I gave him a copy of the note I'd found. I'd figured it out while I was relocating my visitors, so I told him the translation while he wrote it down with the pencil. It was a location, and meeting time a week from now, along with three names to pass the message to.

"My guess is those are gang leaders, not peons," I concluded.

"Cute. Guess we'll have a surprise waiting for them if they act up."

I scowled. "They may think they're being clever, but they're fooling themselves. The Faerie may seem like a submissive, peaceable lot, and they've been patient with the protests this past year, thanks in no small part to Bishop Aiden. But the FFR is making itself too well known. If the Faerie think they're a real threat, they'll unite to protect what's theirs—which your government has made sure they know is their freedom and their equality. You're going to have a nice little war on your hands if you don't do something."

Santry pinched the bridge of his nose with one hand as if to stave off a headache. "This gets better and better. What if it's just a rally?"

I regarded him balefully. When he didn't rescind the question, I said. "There were a lot of Faerie living in that apartment that caught fire, and I noticed no one's ruled out arson yet. I think we're getting past the point where they're going to believe a bunch of people calling for their deaths will stop at motivational chants this time—unless they do the stopping."

"And I left LA for this," he sighed. "You sure about the date? All right, then. Let's talk about the murders. We got an ID on the John Doe—the one we found intact. Lance Pointiers, a dealer in antiquities. He got anything to do with Grace's and your case?"

Antiquities dealer? Did he know about the lance—and die for that knowledge? How much did I tell Santry? Times past, I'd have denied knowing anything about the guy, but I was trying to develop a new attitude with Santry...sort of. Besides, this could affect Grace.

Still, I had nothing helpful to offer, and he might warn me off if I admitted anything, which would tie my claws.

"I don't know. This is the first I've heard of him. Were there signs that anything was stolen? There's an artifacts conference in town. Now that I'm not a suspect in the first murder, do you think the two could be related?"

"Could be. Now that we have an ID, we're checking his hotel room, but the murderer has had time to cover his tracks. God knows what they might have taken. He was shot in the front, close range, but he didn't look like the kind of guy who'd put up a fight or even have the wit to run. His assistant's gone—kidnapped or skipped town, we don't know. We're having a hard time tracking down anyone who knows him. Pointiers was a private dealer and something of a recluse. No next of kin, exclusive clientele. We're trying to contact the

New Orleans police, but they have their hands full right now."

I nodded. Only humans would believe a "once in a century" storm would have the manners to not happen twice within decades, and that their fancy technology could thwart the worst Mother Nature had to offer. That same mentality kept some humans believing they could actually destroy a dragon once and for all. Optimism or stupidity, it annoyed me. At any rate, the devastation left by Hurricane Cody seemed to have also destroyed our lead. "Nothing about him on the 'net? Kind of merchandise, clientele..."

"Just his name, photo, and business address in New Orleans, which is about all they had on him at the conference. Why?"

"Just fishing for connections. What about the other guy?" I asked as long as Santry was being free with his information. Maybe he was trying to develop a new attitude with me, or maybe he was just that tired. He could also be hoping I'd let something slip. I'd have to be sure the local police force didn't follow me around today.

"Jacob Cranston? Run-of-the-mill thug-for-hire. Got a rap sheet as long as your tail, mostly petty stuff—enforcing, theft, harassment. Usually bailed out by someone else's lawyer. No family; we're still looking for friends. Why was Grace trailing him?"

"Harassment case. The client was a little sharper than usual."

Santry grimaced at my non-informative response. "And no theories why someone would try to murder him and pin it on you?"

I gave him a smug grin. "Glad you believe that now, but no. I'm surprised they'd think it would work—anyone who knows me knows I don't like fillet minion."

Thus wounded by my wit, Santry left. The paddy wagon showed up to escort my shell-shocked guests to a nice safe prison cell, and Tracy returned to collect their gear. She shook her head sadly at the pile. Since it was being used for a case, I couldn't ask for it back. However, once she'd left, I took Junior's gun out back and blasted it to slag. It felt good to use my fire.

Then I went and called the hospital. The ICU nurse answered. She must have been the one who saw me earlier that morning. She invited me to call her Lois, then updated me.

"She's not changed since you left, I'm afraid," she told me. "She's not responding to any treatment, and the poison won't leave her system. We don't know why. The Faerie healer is in with her now, but I don't think it's helping much. It's certainly not helping Doctor Sidwell's temper, either."

I grunted. I didn't really care if it sat well with Sidwell unless he was such a jerk that it affected how he treated Grace. I asked Lois about that.

"Oh, don't worry. He may have an ego that stretches to Mars, but he's an excellent physician. He just takes it personally when things aren't in his control, and all this Faerie stuff is way beyond his understanding."

I snorted. I wondered if he and Santry knew each other. They'd probably hit it off.

"Dr. Sidwell is saying she's in a persistent vegetative state. He's waiting for her mother superior to come so they can decide the next steps. The healer said she'd be here early tomorrow."

I fought the urge to snarl in frustration. They should be talking to me. I was the closest thing to family Grace had. Mother Angela was wonderful with people and one of the best Holy Mages in the

Church, but otherwise didn't swim in the deepest of intellectual waters. I doubt she'd understand half of what Dr. Sidwell told her or comprehend the implications of "persistent vegetative state." However, she had trusted Mundane medicine enough to send Sister Grace to Walter Reed for psychiatric treatment when nothing her order could do helped—and it had been the right decision. Would she trust a physician when he says there's no hope, especially after a healer had not been able to cure her?

Suddenly, I had a deadline on this case that threatened to become literal.

No sooner did I hang up than another call came in. The caller ID said, "Anonymous." Probably a phone solicitor wanting to scam me out of my social security number. Boy, were they in for a surprise.

I should have been so lucky.

Instead, a computer-generated voice operating at speeds no human could comprehend but a dragon could make out said, "Grace is almost out of time. We have the cure. Find us the lance. Say nothing to the authorities, secular or spiritual. We will contact you." The call ended, too short for a trace.

So the ones who shot my partner didn't have the lance. That was good news and bad news. Good news because it gave me bargaining power and because, well, they didn't have it for whatever mischief they'd planned. Bad because saving Grace's life meant giving them what they needed for whatever mischief they planned—provided I found it before they did, or Ramada did, or who-ever else was in this scavenger hunt.

Provided I found it before it was too late for Grace.

Maybe if Cambridge found it, I could secure a bargain. Did I trust him, though? I knew about as much about him as I did about Eva. No. I couldn't mention the lance to him. He was a rival now.

I couldn't even ask for help from the police. Why had I been so secretive? I hadn't told Santry about the lance. Now I couldn't, nor could I put anyone else on alert without risking Grace. But if the lance was the real one and it did get smuggled into Faerie?

When I'd gone after the Faerie Lance of Longinus, I'd had the might of the Church helping me. Now, I couldn't even ask Bishop Aiden for advice.

Would my mystery caller know, though?

Who was I kidding? First, they wouldn't have to know. If they discovered me talking to Aiden, they'd assume, and Grace would be dead. Besides, there was no way Aiden would chance such a powerful artifact crossing the Gap and getting infused with magic.

Maybe we could set up a sting?

No. There were mages in the Mundane now. One might even be on my caller's payroll. Bishop Aiden would never take that chance.

If I wanted to save Grace, I was on my own. Fortunately, that was not anything new for me since I'd moved to the Mundane. The heat was on, but dragons had no problem with heat.

I did the only thing I could do. I looked for that lance.

I resumed my research on the Mundane Lance of Longinus and the people so keen on finding it. Two hours later, the only thing I'd accomplished was putting a dent in the wall from twitching my tail in frustration. There were plenty of rumors and conspiracy theories about the current where-abouts of the Lance of Longinus, along with some articles with actual scholarly merit, yet none of them put the lance anywhere in the U.S., let alone Colorado.

Dead end, then. I delved into the backgrounds of my suspects. Like Santry, I didn't find much on Pointiers. I'd have suspected it was a nom de commerce, except that Santry would have run his prints. Maybe he used an alias for his personal life?

Surprisingly enough, Eva Heidler and her brother Weylin were legit people. She'd even been honest about her parents dying when Weylin was young, leaving her to raise him. I found addresses for them in New York, Chicago, Denver... Denver was the latest. Spotty employment, mostly restaurant-type jobs, no record of collecting welfare or unemployment between jobs. Her innocence could have been as fake as her hair, or maybe she had a sugar daddy—or several.

Weylin wasn't registered in any of the local schools. Had Eva followed him from Denver?

As I read, I tried not to kick myself. I hadn't asked enough questions. I could afford to be that sloppy when it was just my life on the line. Not now.

What was Eva's angle on this game? I was pretty certain it hadn't been to set me and Grace up. There were any number of easier ways to do that without getting herself in the line of fire. And she seemed savvy enough to know that getting in a dragon's line of fire was a dangerous thing, in-deed.

I decided to pay her another visit. Naturally, now that I had better questions for her, she was not in her hotel. I took a chance and inquired at the front desk. Interestingly enough, the recep-tionist handed me a note Eva had left for me.

Vern. I'm sorry. I am just so scared. People are being murdered and I don't know if I'll be next. I know you don't trust me, so I'm leaving. Let's just call it even.—Eva

Call it even? She owed me money, not to men-tion Grace's current dire state was her fault.

Even!

Had she abandoned her brother, then, or found him? What about her search for the lance?

Fortunately, the receptionist was a fantasy geek who was only too glad for a chance to talk to an actual dragon. Once I got him to stop talking like an RPG, he told me Eva had left shortly after my visit last night, requesting a Rhyde to the bus station. She hadn't seemed in a particular hurry, he said, nor did she seem as distressed as the note would suggest. No, she didn't mention her brother, a lance, or Cambridge.

"Though I really didn't ask," the receptionist said apologetically. "She was renting by the week and only left a day early. That's not especially unusual."

I thanked him and left. Her scent ended at the curb—probably where she got her Rhyde. I flew to the bus station, sniffed around, and caught vague traces of her, but not enough to know if she took a bus or just stopped there to make it look good.

I went inside and flashed a photo of her that I'd pulled off the internet. However, since I wasn't a cop, the new guy behind the counter didn't feel inclined to give me any information. Shifts had changed since the last bus had left, so there was no one to ask if they'd seen her board.

I thought about the hair coloring and contacts she'd worn for our meeting. A wig and a change of outfit, and no one would recognize her, anyway. Humans in general weren't especially observant, and on this side of town, being too observant could be hazardous for your health.

Chapter Eight:
Despredatores and
Desperate Pleas

Speaking of the bad side of town, I decided it was time to pay a visit to Los Despredatores. If there was a new gang—Brotherhood, whatever—they'd at least know about it. They might even know the ringleaders, size of membership, and claimed neighborhoods.

I found a handful of them in the park, shooting a basketball through a hoop with no net. I waited for Mateo to line up a three-pointer and dove down to snatch the ball before he scored.

There are times when it's gratifying to get cursed at.

"Why aren't you in school?" I demanded.

"Give me a break, drake!" Mateo snapped at me. "It was a half-day. Seriously. Teachers gotta workshop or sumthin'."

I believed him. He'd taken over Los Despreda-tores after the Mishmash incident, when his leader had gotten involved in the concert that had summoned a monster. After that, Wolf's family had moved to Minnesota. That summer, Mateo's mother took off with some guy, and his abuela came back from Mexico to take care of him. Thus, as he liked to complain, he found himself in charge of a gang, but not his own life. When Abuela found out he was failing because of bad attendance, she threatened to return to Mexico, dragging him with her. I'd cheerfully offered to fly him there personally.

Now, he kept a steady C average and was limiting the gang's more objectionable activities to outside school grounds and school hours. Our little hood was growing up at last.

"Give us the ball back, drake. Why you hasslin' us?"

I spun the ball on a claw because I could. "I need information. Sister Grace is in trouble. What have you heard about the Brotherhood of Baal?"

They answered with confusion and catcalls.

"We got the brotherhood, Vern. Now give us the ball!" Eugene jumped up. I easily avoided his grasp with a single wing flap. I didn't even lose balance of the spinning ball.

"Not 'ball,' Moron." I wasn't insulting him. That was his gang name. Someone had called him that, and he thought it was clever. Who was going to report that they got beat up by a Moron? That was one way to "flip the script."

I added, "I mean 'Baal,'" like the ancient Egyptian god."

"Like on Stargate?" Alberto said. He'd taken the break to go put his arms around Lisabel. I guess they'd made up again. "That dude's bad news!"

"Yes, thank you!" I said as his compatriots jeered at him and he responded that Samantha Carter was hot. Lisabel punched his arm and stalked away.

"Either way, don' change my answer," Eugene argued. "Don't know them. Don't care. Give us our ball."

The others nodded in agreement—except for Alberto who was digging himself in deeper by trying to explain to Lisabel that Sam Carter was an "old broad in this old TV show."

I tossed it into the air and caught it with a back claw. "What about the Fellowship of the Fourth Reich? I know they're at MLK High. Any at LLH?"

The mood shifted. Los Despredatores looked at each other and the ground. Fists clenched, but it was the sign of helpless rage. That was not good.

Mateo said, "Yeah. We don't mess with them."

"'Cause they ain't started nuthin' with us yet!" Moron interjected. Mateo shouted for him to shut up.

"So they're at your school, but keeping a low profile?" I asked.

Mateo answered. "Mostly insults, some shoving. Swirlies. Usual bullying stuff. We're keeping it cool. I'm trying to graduate, Vern, you know? Besides, these guys got wicked hardware."

"I've seen. Some whitefaces paid me a visit. I chucked them in the dumpster."

"Guns?" Moron asked, greed shining in his eyes. I could see he'd be my next project.

"The clowns. You don't go snooping in my place. You know that."

Despite all the times that I'd handed their tails to them, they still looked at me with renewed respect.

The Moron asked the question that would endear me to him forever. "That when they hurt Sister Grace? You want us to get some justice?"

Bless you, Eugene. You are definitely my next project. "I don't know who hurt Grace. Whoever it was used a poison dart from a high-powered tranquilizer gun. Heard anything about that?"

It was a long shot, pardon the pun, but a chance not taken was a loss given.

All I got were shrugs and headshakes.

I sighed. "Okay. How about the scuttlebutt on the FFR activities? They seem excited about anything?

"You ma—" Moron started on reflex. Then he caught my glare and mashed his lips shut. He was learning, albeit slowly.

"They're strutting around more," Albert offered from where he now sat next to Lisabel, his hand on her knee—a partial reconciliation, I supposed. "Terry Block actually wore his whiteface to school. If Mateo hadn't ordered us to cool it, I'd have helped him wash it off in the toilet. Reese suspended him. He ain't effin' around with that racist shit."

"I was in the office," Mateo added. "Terry was like, amused. I mean, almost triumphant. He said the time was coming when 'they' would lead them in revolution, and he was gonna make Principal Reese top of his hit list. He got an extra week for that."

"Who's 'they'?" I asked.

"Dunno. But he made them sound like hot stuff. Like Nazi Christmas."

"Nazis don't have Christmas!" Moron said. "They're like, atheist or obnostic or something."

"That's communists, Moron," Alberto retorted. "And the only one who's 'obnostic' is you. Shit, I feel dumber just listening to you."

"Yeah? Well, who's got the hots for some old broad from the 90s?"

The others were getting restless. One asked, "Come on, Vern. Can we have our ball? Otherwise, I'm gonna go have a hit."

"Have you done your homework?" I asked them all.

That earned me howls of protests, but I was just razzing them. I was not their keeper. I did enough babysitting for the Costas.

"Fine. If you hear anything, let me know," I told them.

"Vern," Mateo said, "seriously, what kind of weapons?"

I gave him a list from AK to nunchucks.

Mateo frowned. "That's basic, drake. I've heard-tell they got better stuff than that."

"Tranquilizer gun?" I asked.

He shrugged, but said, "I saw a grenade at the office. Missus Payne was a little freaked when Reese was putting it in the safe. Bet it came from Block. Be careful, Vern."

"If anybody gonna take you down, it's us," Alberto added. The others cheered in agreement. Their bravado was so cute, the little snacks.

I tossed the ball in the air and gave it a calculated smack with my tail. It sailed into the basket.

A couple of the girls cheered from the benches, but the guys shouted protests. I left them arguing whether using a tail was a legit move, or if that only counted in soccer.

So far, I was two for zero. Maybe I could sniff something out at the antiquities conference.

The conference was held at the Los Lagos Fine Arts Center. I had a real love-hate relationship with this spot. On the one hand, I got into big trouble here my first couple of months in the Mundane when I innocently tried to stop a pickpocket and ended up getting arrested instead. On the other hand, I'd made my first set of friends—a gaming group led by the comic bookstore owner in the plaza. I dropped by the store to say hi to Owen, the only one left in the area of the original group.

Owen had been on our side through the whole anti-Faerie ordeal. In fact, when the protests started, he'd changed his display to X-Men and other comics that dealt with racism and oppression. His reward was a smashed display window and destroyed merchandise. And what did he say? "Some of the comics were stolen. I can only hope they get read and understood."

Owen was a good guy. I could use a few minutes with a good guy. Not to mention, he might have some useful gossip about the business side of the city.

A sign on the door declared it closed for ComiCon.

I headed across the plaza, counting "one, Hail Mary, two, Hail Mary," a habit I'd picked up from Grace for helping keep my temper. Miraculously, it worked. At eight-Hail Mary, I entered the building and approached the desk with a calm and friendly attitude.

Too bad no one noticed.

The receptionist took one look at me and screamed, "Dragon!"

Behind her, through the half-opened doors, I saw the trade show erupt into turmoil. Immediately, people took up her call, adding adjectives and verbs that did not describe my stationary, befuddled state but rather painted me as on the rampage. The only rampage was happening in that room.

People started screaming and running to the back exit. Others threw tarps over their displays. I wasn't sure which was more insulting. The receptionist dashed through the door, shutting them behind her. I heard scraping as people shoved tables against them as a barricade.

I hadn't even said "hello," much less explained that I only wanted to talk to the organizer.

I sat there, gaping, listening to the chaos, and trying to decide what my next move should be, when two security guards came barreling down the hall. Fortunately, they were locals—and one was Kel.

"Jeez, Vern! What are you doing here?" he asked, annoyed.

I took one last look at the doors, where I now heard shallow frightened breathing. I guess a few had decided to stick around and protect their treasures against my imagined raid.

I turned my back on them. One, Hail Mary...

I said, "I could ask you the same question. Are you moonlighting or something?"

With a jerk of his head, Kel led me back outside while his compatriots dealt with chaos in the trade showroom. We left as they were tapping on the door and trying to convince the others behind it that they were not me disguising my voice to get in.

I hadn't spoken a word. I hadn't even gotten past the reception desk. That had to be a new record.

Kel was talking. "Sonya's expecting and the arts center needed extra security for the show. So, I figured it'd be easy cash. Of course, I also know the people a little better, so Santry asked me to question them. What are you doing here?"

"I wanted to ask the organizers some questions. So did you know Pointiers?" I asked.

"Nah. He didn't have a booth. Folks said he attended some of the panels, but he doesn't say much. All about business. He's got a great rep, though. If someone wants to find something specific, they say he's the one to go to. If it exists, he'll find it."

I so badly wanted to ask about the lance.

"Look, Vern, I promised I'd share what I learn, okay? You really shouldn't be traipsing around, not when people think you killed that guy."

"I thought Santry cleared me!"

"But we still haven't caught the murderer. Besides, you must have seen the news."

Fewmets! I forgot about McGrue. And the local TV station was right next door to the arts center, where I'd just started a panic by "returning to the scene of the crime." In fact, I wouldn't be surprised if they were mobilizing a film crew and reporter as we spoke.

"This day gets better and better," I grumbled.

"How's Sister Grace?" Kel asked.

"Not good. She needs an antidote, and I'm running out of leads."

Kel shook his head sadly. "That stinks. I wish I had something to offer. But I think it's best you clear out now."

"Yeah, fine." Another dead end. All I'd managed to do was glance at the registration list. At least it went A through Q. I didn't see any Heidlers, but there was a Wolfgang Hayden below Pointiers name. Pointiers name had been crossed out with a teary face beside it.

"Before I do, can you check out a Wolfgang Hayden? His name was on the registration list but out of alphabetical order. It was below Pointiers. Maybe he was an assistant?"

"Sure, I can check."

"Thanks. Also, you might want to question the receptionist. I think she may have known Pointiers more than professionally. Could have just been a crush, but..." I shrugged my wings.

Kel blinked at me. "How would you know that?"

"Just something I picked up," I said.

We said our goodbyes, being extra friendly in case someone was recording us from the window. Then, with nothing better to do, I cased the area, then flew a search grid around the city, trying to sniff out the lance, the poisons that were killing Grace, anything, but the day was hot and heavy, with an upper high-pressure front keeping in all the pollution and smells of Los Lagos—too many scents to sort through. The only thing I managed to find was one of my vandal visitors—he'd gone to church. That wasn't good news: the minister at First Family Congregation believed all magic was of the Devil. He'd probably supported the "crusade" against the Faerie.

Another dead end.

Our Lady of Sorrows was only a block away. Time to regroup.

It was quiet this late in the afternoon. I had the entire church to myself, but I knelt in the side aisle, where there was a statue of Our Lady of Sorrows. Based on a Spanish sculpture of the Virgin Mother holding a crucified Jesus in her lap, she wore the saddest expression I'd ever seen. I felt like the artist understood pain. For some reason, that comforted me.

I blew a small flame to one of the many candles in the racks in front of the statue and settled myself into a reverent pose.

Lord, you blessed me at the dawn of the Earth with wisdom beyond any mortal's. Thanks to St. George, most of that's gone now, but I'm not holding that against You. You and I both know what could happen if that lance gets to Faerie, but Grace...

I couldn't form any words.

What I wanted to do was howl, full-throated and uncontrolled. I wanted Los Lagos—I wanted all the worlds, Mundane and Faerie—to know my rage against God and Man who conspired to bring me so low, to make me dependent on them, then to make themselves so dear to me.

To make me so afraid that I no longer had what it took to protect them.

I don't know how long I was there, lost in my emotions, until I heard a tiny, "Excuse me?" I willed my face to lose its grimace and my eyes to open.

A sister stood beside me, her pale complexion and wide eyes making her look too young to have taken vows (in the Mundane Church, anyway). She had to have been new and from somewhere far away. I wondered if the local bishop was breaking her in slowly; this side of town didn't have a lot of Magical residents.

Welcome to Los Lagos, kid.

She trembled slightly, and by the way her eyes flickered from me to the statue of Mary I was posed under, it was obvious she was thinking Revelation. Nonetheless, she had the grace—and the guts—to swallow down her misgivings and ask, "Please, can I help you?"

With that question, my anger washed away, replaced by weariness. "No, sister," I said, rising slowly so as to not frighten her further, "there's only one who can help me now. Just pray for me. Pray for us all."

I headed to the Colt's Hoof. Some of my contacts should be there. Besides, I needed a drink.

Chapter Nine:
It's All Fun and Games
Until Someone Loses a Life

"So what'd ya go and kill that guy for, Vern?"

I closed my eyes, poured the rest of my Killian into my mouth, and swallowed. It was the third time in an hour I'd been asked that question. It seemed everyone wanted to remind me that I'd been accused of murder, and (as usual) found guilty in the Court of Public Opinion. Worse, no one so far had had any information that could help me find the real murderers or the people who'd hurt Grace or the lance, which I couldn't even mention in case I was being followed by someone wiser and more skilled than Junior had been. If this kept up, I was going to abandon my quest for information and surrender myself to about five gallons of ethanol for a real binge.

I told my latest companion, "I didn't, Lenny. Someone beat me to it."

Lenny was your standard low-class inform-ant—did fewer drugs than he claimed, but nonetheless sold some to pay for his habit, on the edge of everything, but never actually in. Good ears, good eyes, good sense of self-preservation. He usually didn't give me information at the Hoof, but today, he seemed willing to make an excep-tion, which meant the information he had was widely known. "Yeah? Well, there's some weird shit going on where you's concerned. You know there's a price on your head, but anyone who offs you before the 17th is a dead man?"

A price on my head? Just what I needed: an-other wrinkle.

"The 17th, hm?" That was the day of the "rally." "So who's after me this time?" I stuck money in his jacket pocket with my tail.

"Don't know, fer sure," he said, sticking his hand in his pocket to count the bills. I knew he liked fives, neatly folded. "Some say it's the FFR Some say the Unseelie crew is back. Some say it's some fereigners I ain't never heard of. Columbi-ans, maybe. I know a red-haired chick's been doing the talkin'." He grinned a salacious smile.

"Redhead, huh? Did you pick her pocket or pinch her butt?" His smile could have indicated either.

But he surprised me with a sigh. "Neither. She had a coupla toughs with her. You know, the kind that hang back acting all uninvolved until you try a little innocent get-to-know-you, and suddenly, they smash your face in the pavement?"

Like I said, good sense of survival. "So you didn't talk to her?"

"No, I did. Sort of. I had just finished transacting some business and was savoring the moment."

Translation: He'd sold some drugs and was getting high on what he'd kept for himself.

"...when this vision with red hair and the most amazing knockers came up to me and told me it wasn't my fault that I was whatever-the-heck she thought was wrong with me. At first, I thought she was a social worker 'cept no social worker would be walking around the neighborhood with toughs or showing off her knockers so well."

"I like how you prioritized her goons over her attributes."

"I ain't stupid. But she had all the attributes, if you know what I mean."

"I can guess, and it's disgusting coming from you. Continue."

"Whatever. Anyway, she started giving me the usual crap about how it ain't my fault and the gov'mint's hosed and how I deserve better. So I thought she might be wanting me to vote or something and I didn't even know there was an election. But then, then she starts talking trash about the Faerie and the wetbacks and the Jews and I was kind of like, 'What the hell?' but the way she talked was so compelling. She's a believer, Vern."

"Oh?"

"Yeah, like it was the freaking Second Coming. She said some guy was going to unite the righteous race and people like me would be the masters overall. Sounded good on paper, I suppose, but I don't need that kind of responsibility, you know."

I had to admire how Lenny knew his limits. "Righteous race?"

I looked at my tipsy tattletale: Human, blond hair, blue eyes. Square enough jaw if he hadn't been so skinny from the drugs.

"Did she happen to mention what they planned to do with the not-so-righteous races?"

He shrugged. "I dunno. I was starting to lose track of the conversation."

"Because you were high?"

"She might have been trippin' herself. She invited me to a rally, said the Nine furries were coming."

"Nine furries? Or *mein Führer*?"

Lenny paused with his drink halfway to his mouth. "Whoa! Yeah, that's even more out there. Hitler'd be like a hundred or something. Besides, he's dead. Unless... Are there like necromancers or something that would bring him back?"

Before I could argue his math or his logic, one of the customers near the door screamed with surprise.

Big Guns, his shaved head sweating, staggered into the bar. He banged into a table, upsetting drinks and eliciting more shrieks, then lurched my way. As he got to the bar, he fell to his knees and handed me a package. The "FARISLAR" tattoo shone darkly against his pale knuckles.

"I'm sorry," he gasped. "I didn't realize... Stop them. Tell them I'm sorry..." He collapsed fully and I saw the swastika on his jacket back was saturated with his own blood.

"Call an ambulance!" I ordered, even though I didn't think he had that kind of time. As others sprang into action, I dashed out of the bar.

I'm sure everyone thought I was going after his attackers, but they weren't around. I'd have heard them. Rick must have lost them or escaped. Maybe they'd left him for dead. I don't know how he made it across the room much less from wherever he'd been left. Either way, I hoped this was a sign he was turning his life around. If he lived. If not, well, God was a good judge of character.

I headed to the roof. I had a pretty good idea what was in the package; if so, my prayers had been answered, or I may have an even more painful decision ahead of me.

I peeled back the brown paper and pushed aside the straw packing. Of course, it wasn't the antidote. That would have been too easy. I sniffed at the spear, tasted the wood. My claws extended, crinkling the paper.

This wasn't fair, God!

I shook myself. Fine. If the cards were stacked against me, I would be glad to cheat a little.

I headed down the street to the local courier service. The world wanted to star me in Maltese Falcon; fine, but I was changing the script.

I got home, left messages for Cambridge Ramada and Eva Heidler, and waited for my mysterious caller. "I don't have the lance, but I know where it is. I want the antidote and the murderers brought to me tomorrow morning at 8 a.m. or no deal," I told the recorder and hung up before it could. I didn't need a trace. Lenny had told me who it was. I kenneled the dogs and settled down to wait.

I don't know if it was the stress or maybe the fact that I hadn't eaten in 24 hours, but I nodded off somewhere in the middle of the night. I woke up to the slap of meat as someone once again drugged the dogs. I hoped they were just tranquilizers. I did not need to explain sick dogs to our friend on top of everything else.

The dawn light peeked through the windows, casting lines of orange light on the floor. At least I'd managed to get most of a night's sleep. I counted my blessings as I padded quietly to the kitchen for a snack before my would-be attacker broke in. Didn't want to break my promise to Kel not to eat any suspects, after all.

He busted in to find me lying by the table, gnawing on a large ham. "You're early, Weylin," I commented, feigning obliviousness to the laser sight tickling my scales. "The lance isn't here, and you won't get it if you kill me now; so don't make the same mistake your whiteface minions did. Sit down and wait, Unless, of course, you don't have the antidote or the names of the murderers. In that case, you've got a couple of hours to fetch them for me. Otherwise, put that thing down and stay calm or you'll never see the lance."

Weylin opened his mouth to speak, closed it, then pulled up a chair in resignation, keeping it well out of my range, even that of my tail. He refused food but took an unopened can of soda.

It must have been later than I'd realized because I finished my snack and was just beginning to unnerve him with my Sphinx-like stare when we heard a knock and Eva let herself in with a tentative, "Vern...?"

When she saw my other guest, her face went into an amusing series of surprise, confusion, and indecision, before pasting on a look of delight. "Vern, you found him!"

She was good. I'd give her that.

"Cut the act, Eva. He was never lost, and you know it as well as I. Sit down and stay quiet. We've got one more guest coming, then I want the antidote, some names, and some answers, in that order. I'll give the lance to whomever I believe the most."

"You have the lance?"

"Not with me. I'm not stupid—look it up on my website. A penitent FFR gave it to me in a bar— I'm sure one or more of you know that. I took the liberty of mailing it to myself. It's in a safe place for now—and not in my lair, so please don't bother looking. Again, I'm smarter than that. I'll share its whereabouts—after our next guest arrives."

Eva shared a glance at Weylin, who shrugged. With one of her own, she pulled up a chair and sat. I noticed that she did not sit near her brother, but at an angle and nearer the door. Smart cookie, that one.

At 10 to eight, Ramada arrived without Junior. He looked from me to my guests and let out his signature snicker. "I see you've been busy. Good morning, Miz Heidler. May I assume that this is your wayward brother, Weylin? Vern, my congratulations. Are there others we should expect?"

"Not unless Junior is joining us? I don't smell him around, but maybe he bathed?"

"Heh hemm. No. I'm afraid I've engaged him in other activities."

Covering the lair from a distance, no doubt. That was fine by me. I also had backup on the way.

I didn't invite Ramada to sit. I wasn't sure my thrift store chairs were up to the challenge. He seemed content to stand.

I stood, stretched, and addressed my merry little party. "First off, who has the antidote?"

Everyone looked at everyone else. Finally, Cambridge spoke. "I do not even know the nature of the poison, but as I'd said earlier, I will ensure my client secures the best care possible for your partner. If there is a cure, you will have it."

"I'm not showing you anything until I see the lance," Weylin muttered.

Eva just looked innocent and confused. Did she ever break character?

Two strikes and a maybe. "All right. We'll table that, but no antidote, no lance. Let's talk murders. What's the story with Cranston?"

"He was one of mine, I'm afraid," Cambridge said, heaving a sigh instead of his usual asthmatic snicker. "Problem with hiring the local help. He was supposed to put pressure on Miss Heidler here, show her the wisdom of relinquishing the lance to my client. At the same time, he was supposed to be using his contacts to find young Weylin here. I didn't anticipate his lascivious nature nor expect Miss Heidler to turn the tables on us."

"Well?" I prompted Eva.

"All right," she looked at her hands, even now playing demure. "I didn't have the lance. I didn't know where Weylin was—we got separated after..."

"After one of you killed Pointiers?"

"It wasn't like that!" Weylin said. "He'd promised me the lance. He'd brought it here for me. He even demanded extra money. Then he suddenly decided to renege on our deal, the little—" He swore in German. Like I wouldn't understand his anti-Semitic remarks.

Eva glanced up sharply and hissed, but it was too late. He'd confirmed my suspicions. If Lenny had known his information was so accurate, he'd probably have charged more.

I shrugged my wings, feigning nonchalance. "So you shot him. Fine. What about Cranston? Why make it look like me?"

Brother and sister exchanged bewildered looks. One or both of them was acting.

I was so tired. I'd let Santry sort that part out.

"Why risk killing for it?" I asked in my best long-suffering voice. "There are three known lances making claims to be the Lance of Destiny. You know this one's probably fake?"

"It is the real one! We have done the research—Pointiers and Eva and I. This is the lance used by Longinus to pierce Christ and which our—"

"Weylin, shut up!" Eva shouted. "He does not need to know!" Then, she turned to me, her eyes pleading and innocent. "Please, Vern, please. We are certain it's the real one; even more, those from whom we were stealing it know it's the real one. They're the real enemy here. And he's in their employ!" She pointed theatrically in Ramada's direction, but he only chuckled.

I didn't say anything to call attention to her slip. Pointiers was a legit dealer. He would not be part of a theft, and Weylin had just said they'd hired Pointiers to bring the lance to them. Instead, I watched, my expression neutral. I only needed a couple of minutes more.

She filled the silence. "Don't you understand? They're the ones who hurt Sister Grace. After what you told me, Vern, I know we have to spirit the lance away. I wish I had an antidote, I really do. But isn't it more important that we get the lance away from here? I've been watching the news. I know there's a big Fourth Reich cell here. They're behind all that, too, don't you see? Help us, Vern. Give us the lance. We'll escape to Faerie, have it destroyed—"

Her solilo-plea was interrupted by a knock on the door. The courier, right on time. I moseyed to the door, everyone following close behind me. Weylin, at least, had the sense to hide his gun behind his back.

The courier had been told to expect a dragon at the door, but his eyes went wide, nonetheless. Of course, they flickered toward Eva. Way to hurt my pride.

I took the package between my teeth so no one would be tempted to wrest it from me. "Pay the nice man, Eva," I instructed through my mouthful.

Despite her feigned tension, she managed to "Tuh!"

Ramada, chuckling all the while, paid the delivery fee and tip.

They gathered around the table as I ripped apart the packaging. They began oohing and awing at once.

"It's amazing!" Ramada murmured.

"It's beautiful!" Eva breathed.

"It's ours," Weylin hissed.

"It's fake." I sing-songed.

They turned to me in surprise. I rolled my eyes. "You can't fool this nose. The blood staining the shaft? Not more than 500 years old. The shaft itself is acer plantanoides. They didn't have Olmsted Norway Maples in the Roman Empire. You're looking at a bona fide copy—no power potential whatsoever."

Eva gave a small gasp. Weylin opened and closed his mouth several times, but nothing came out.

Ramada sighed deep in his throat. It came out as a wheeze. "A shame, a shame. Nonetheless, my employer is more interested in the historical content. As I am the one most likely to obtain an antidote, may I assume the prize goes to me?"

"No!" the other two shouted in desperate unison.

On cue, sirens began to wail outside.

"Actually, I think the police will have to decide that..." I said as uniformed officers burst into my lair, guns drawn.

Weylin swung his gun from behind his back, but I knocked it out of his hands before he could fire it. That was all the time Eva needed to grab the lance and run. I trampled over Weylin as I dashed for her. She ran through the double doors that led to the lair and through the maze of boxes and shelves, seeking an exit.

Unfortunately for her, she got as far as the locked back door that led to the dumpsters. She only had time to look at the window which stood tantalizingly open from her brother's earlier entrance before I lashed out with my tail and pulled the lance from her hands. Behind us, we heard the police struggling with Weylin.

"Wait!" she exclaimed.

Slowly, she pulled something out of her purse. "Antidote."

The vial shone dully in the light from the window. I was mesmerized, the commotion behind us forgotten.

She spoke beguilingly. "It doesn't matter if the lance is fake; it's still worth a fortune. But you don't care about that, do you? You have a greater treasure—your friend the nun. Give me the lance; tell the police I'm an innocent bystander. I'm your client, remember? Do it, and the antidote's yours." She swirled the cloudy liquid temptingly.

And I was tempted. God forgive me, even when I knew she was a liar and evil to the core, I was tempted. And it made me furious.

My hesitation emboldened her. She stepped toward me.

I unfurled my wings with a snap, and I reared into my most aggressive stance. She fell back with a tight scream.

"Forget it, Eva Heidler—or should I say, Führer-wanna-be Miss Hitler?"

She gasped, whether to protest or monologue, I didn't know, but I wasn't giving her a chance to speak. If I never heard her voice again, it'd been too soon.

"You did a great job covering your tracks, but like an overconfident hack, you forgot about your names. Heidler—a derivative of Hitler. And Weylin—son of the wolf, son of Adolf, which also means wolf? Your parents were as bad as Ramada's. You're the one the skinheads are planning the rally for. Were you going to use the lance to inspire them to massacre?"

She recovered from her surprise quickly. Her expression and tone turned nasty. Now I saw the real Eva.

"I don't have to answer to you. I'm a Mundane. I don't have to follow cliché." But behind her, brother Weylin was already spilling his guts about their glorious plan, interspersed with propaganda and insults for the "Faerie-loving" coppers who were cuffing him as he ranted. I'd have laughed if the stakes weren't so high.

"Give it up, Eva," I pushed. "Give me the antidote. Do you really want to add another murder to your list of crimes?"

"Please! You think my people don't know where I am? Arrest me! Kill me! Make me a martyr. She's just Faerie filth like you." With a snarl, she spun and threw the vile out the window. I heard it shatter against the dumpsters.

With a roar, I gave myself to my rage. I slammed the lance on the ground, shattering it in my fury, then loosed a stream of fire and set it ablaze.

Eva screamed and threw herself at me. I knocked her aside. I heard Santry shouting, but his words meant nothing. I breathed fire upon the lance until even the cement floor cracked and crumbled. I breathed fire upon it until it was nothing but ash.

I breathed fire upon it knowing I had just killed my partner—and my best friend.

When at last the fire in my belly and my heart had spent itself, I became aware of Santry's shouts. "What the hell were you doing? That was evidence!"

"That was a weapon. Haven't you heard the street buzz? The new Hitler was coming and he— or she—" I threw a nasty look at Eva "—was bringing a weapon of Mundane magic to lead them in their cause. Get enough SS wannabes believing that Lance makes them invincible, and you've got an army of single-minded fanatics who think they can't die. And that's just what would have happened with a fake. I just did you a favor, Santry. I just did this whole damn world a favor."

I turned to Eva, "Because you know what, *mein führerin?* That was the genuine article. I lied."

With a scream, she launched herself at me. I swatted her Santry's way and turned my back on them both as she struggled against him.

"I'm going to see Grace. Lock up when you're done here, Santry. I'll be by the station after..."

I didn't finish my statement.

Chapter Ten:
The Greater Treasure

I sat on my haunches in Grace's crowded room,
my tail curled tightly about me to keep it from
thrashing and knocking into any of the equipment. I'd been sent to the corner to recite silent
Hail Marys while Dr. Do-Little Sidwell did his best
to talk Mother Superior Angela into turning everything off, and Father Rich argued for keeping
everything on.

"There's nothing it can do for her anymore. We
haven't been able to flush the poison or the extra
iron out of her system. We have no antidote. Your
healer failed." Sid-unwell listed every failure like
a nail in Grace's coffin.

I clamped my jaws shut. I'd told them to flush
the iron out of her system the first time I'd arrived.
Dr. Doubting Thomas had been too slow to order
the procedure. What would a dragon know about
medicine? Never mind "Wisdom of the ages,

eternities of experience." Never mind millennia that I'd seen this in our Great War...

I would not seek revenge. *Lead me not into temptation...*

"She's in a persistent vegetative state," the doc repeated again, as if the words were some kind of mantra. Now his only contribution seemed to be to toll the bell of hopelessness. "She is brain dead."

"You can't know that!" Father Rich interrupted.

"She's not," Mother Angela whispered. Telepathy was extremely rare in Faerie, but she was one of the few that had the ability to detect thoughts and emotions in general, though not in detail. "But her mind is failing with her body. We need a cure."

"And there is none." Sidwell concluded authoritatively. "That woman was just teasing your dragon."

"Then we need a miracle," she said, and wandered away from both men, ignoring the two men who argued over Grace's mortal fate. She looked at the equipment and shivered.

She caught me watching her and came to stand beside me, resting her hand on my shoulder just above the wing joints. "This isn't your fault. You brought Sister Grace back to herself when no one else could, not in Faerie or the Mundane. St. George gave you to us, and it has been a blessing."

I shrugged. I didn't feel like a blessing. I couldn't help thinking if it hadn't been for St. George, Grace would be alive and I would be back to my former glory, safe in my mountain home, my only worries keeping my stuff safe from treasure hunters and my skin safe from alchemists—

Wait! What if...?

Suddenly, I was filled with a hope so strong it hurt. Trembling against that hope, I furled my scales and pierced my skin with my claw.

Mother Superior looked at me with dawning comprehension. "I didn't think you—"

"Just pray." I placed the blood upon Grace's chapped lips, careful of the ventilator.

"Vern, what are you doing?" Father asked even as the doctor yelled at me to get away from his patient. I ignored them both, watching my friend intently as I prayed with all my being.

Please, God. Give me this one. It would be the best revenge.

The blood spread and soaked in, and her lips healed and smoothed as we watched.

Mother Angela gave a small hopeful cry. "She needs more, much more. We have to get it into all of her!"

"Give me a syringe!" I yelled at the doctor.

"What? What could you possibly want...?" But Father Rich was already out of the room asking the nurse, the parishioner who talked with me yesterday. Lois came in with an empty needle and at my direction, plunged it into a vein in my wing. That piercing was the sweetest sensation I'd felt in centuries.

"Are you out of your mind?" Doctor Still-in-my-way came out of his momentary surprise and ran to the IV, protecting it with his body. He was fast on the uptake at any rate. "I will not let you do this!"

"You said she was dying!" I argued. "You were ready to give up and let her die!"

"But I wasn't going to try to kill her. I will not stand by and willingly let this happen!"

"Fine!" I snarled and lunged at him over Grace's body. He yelped and backed hastily away, managing to just miss knocking over the no-longer-used dialysis machine then ducking behind it for cover. Rearing over him, I kept him cornered. "Consider yourself under duress."

I looked over my shoulder at Lois. "Do it."

"Please," added Mother Superior.

Avoiding the doctor's eyes, she put the needle into the IV and pushed the plunger home.

We watched with our breaths held.

Grace began to convulse.

"Told you!" the doctor shouted. He pushed the machine aside and began shouting instructions to the nurse. Of course, he wanted to help now.

I ignored him and went to Grace, holding her steady with my arms and tail. "Come on, Grace," I growled. "Don't do this to me. I'm a dragon, remember? Don't make me look bad in front of the Meat."

Suddenly, she was still. There was no sound but the drone of the flat-lined EKG. Dr. Sidwell glared at us accusingly.

"Wait for it..." I murmured.

Suddenly, Grace arched as her body gave a huge gasp. The EKG began to beep in time with a normal heartbeat, and Grace began to fight the ventilator. With happy tears stinging her eyes, the nurse pulled it out.

Faerie. They never miss a cliché.

Grace opened her eyes and took everything in: the equipment, the doctor now fighting his own shock and scrambling to look doctorish while he took her pulse. The nurse and Mother Superior crying happy tears while Father tried to hold back his. Me. I tried to give her an "It's about time" look, but if dragons cried, I'd probably be sobbing with relief.

She glanced at the IV, still pink from my blood. "I didn't know you could do that," she said hoarsely.

That was my nun—so clever. "I haven't been able to since St. George," I told her. "Guess you're too important to die."

"And you're too stubborn to let me." She gave me a weak grin.

The doctor was looking over the readouts on the machines, all, no doubt, returning to a healthy normal. "I... I don't believe this," he said.

I snorted. Grace raised a brow, but I didn't explain. Her eyes were already drifting shut. I set my chin on her stomach and she rubbed the top of my head sleepily. I closed my eyes, too, content for the first time in days.

The doctor was talking about what a treasure my healing blood would be. I didn't know if it was a one-time thing, a true miracle, or if I'd gotten that power back. At the moment, I didn't care.

I'd already regained the greater treasure.

More Trouble for Your Favorite Drake

Ready for the next adventure? Get Siren Spell on Amazon.

You can also follow the series on Amazon. There, you'll find all the stories published thus far. I'm working hard to keep a regular stream, so check back often!

Keep in Touch

If you want to learn about future books, please

- Sign up for my newsletter. https://fabi-anspace.substack.com/subscribe for extra Vern stories, updates and a free book!
- Visit my website (https://karinafa-bian.com)
- Follow me on Facebook: https://www.fa-cebook.com/Karina-Fabian-Speculative-Fiction-with-a-Grin-2233839790277963
- Follow **Vern** on Facebook: https://www.facebook.com/DragonEyePI

Acknowledgements

First, I have to thank everyone that contributed to the original story: Chris Speakman, Pamela Luther, Ellen Gable Hrkach, Lincoln Chrisler, and Tim Marquiz. And of course, my wonderful husband Rob, who is an inspiration and my idea man.

For this version, I have Cesar Chacon to thank for suggesting the rewrite and Rena Shannon for finding all the typos and making some great suggestions. As always, many thanks to all of you who continue to love Vern as much as I do – and maybe even as much as he loves himself!

About the Story & the Author

I wrote the original Greater Treasures back in 2013, after watching the Maltese Falcon because I just loved Vern's noir voice and I wanted him in a grim adventure. I was also inspired by the original cover, which I'd found on a premade cover website by Sarah-Jane Lehoux.

Since that time, however, a lot about him and the universe he lives in has changed, and Cesar Chacon encouraged me to broaden and update the story. This is the version you read now. I'm so glad I took his advice, and I hope you will be, too.

I am writing one to three books a year which I publish under Laser Cow Press. They're usually a DragonEye, a Space Traipse, and one more of whatever catches my fancy. You can find my works at http://karinafabian.com or sign up for my newsletter at https://sendfox.com/fabianspace.

There's More Fun in FabianSpace!

Thank you for buying this book. If you enjoyed it, click to see the others in this series or discover one of the other worlds of FabianSpace.

Science Fiction

Space Traipse: Hold My Beer: Redneck ingenuity and common sense in a Star Trek-ish universe. Enjoy the adventures of the *HMB Impulsive*.

The Rescue Sisters: Intrepid women doing dangerous missions in space for the love of God and humankind.

The Old Man and the Void: Dex is a relic hunter on the edge of the black hole, desperate for the catch of a lifetime.

Jovian Heat: As the next Great Storm of Jupiter rises, Cass must find the father of a baby in peril—but the father died before the child was conceived.

Fantasy

DragonEye Story: Vern's a snarky dragon on the wrong side of the Interdimensional Gap, solving crimes, battling evil, and saving the universes on an all-too-regular basis.

Madness of Kanaan: Deryl isn't crazy; he's psychic, and aliens of two worlds thinks he can save them. Maybe he can—but can he regain his sanity in the process?

Horror

Neeta Lyffe, Zombie Exterminator: Neeta's an average exterminator, taking out bugs, rodents, and the undead. Can she keep her friends alive, pay her bills, and find romance?

Frightliner and Other Tales of the Supernatural (with Colleen Drippé): Truck-driving vampires terrorizing the road, Southern women doing what needs doing, a zombie wedding—a great story collection for horror lovers.

www.ingramcontent.com/pod-product-compliance
Lightning Source LLC
Chambersburg PA
CBHW071603180626
46819CB00002B/114